GW00481792

STRONG TEA

Strong Tea

BY

JOHN B. KEANE

THE MERCIER PRESS
4 BRIDGE STREET, CORK

First published in the Netherlands
By The Mercier Press
summer 1963
© J.B. Keane

Reprinted 1976

ISBN 0 85342 255 9

Thanks are due to the proprietors
of Independent Newspapers Ltd. for
permission to include many of the
following articles.

Reprinted Photo-Litho in the Republic of Ireland

INDEX

ONE

STRONG TEA

'That our enemies might be drinking
bogwater when we'll be drinking tea!'
ANON

THE above wish, at first reading, may appear to be lacking in basic Christian principles, but familiarity with the subject will disclose that 'bogwater' in this instance is the name given by connoisseurs to tea beverages which fall short of requisite standards.

The gravity of this malediction – and a curse it is – would seem to be without parallel in the annals of ill-will for to wish weak tea upon a man is worse than wishing him no tea at all, and if a family is unfortunate enough to earn the reputation of weak tea, a generation may pass before the awful slur is wiped away, and even then a man's children are not safe from the scathing tongues of those who like to resurrect unwelcome skeletons.

Now that the New Year is under weigh and most of us are struggling valiantly to maintain our commendable resolutions, I beg permission to make a suggestion to housewives and others who have charge of teapots, tea-caddies and kettles. I want them to resolve, even at this late stage, that courage and generosity will prevail when the teapot is rinsed out and the kettle nearing the boil. I want them to exhibit contrition for their past misdeeds by putting an extra spoon of tea in the pot and I want them to ensure that the quality of the blend in question will be above suspicion. We have enough to put up with in this maddening era without having to endure the frustrating privations which arise from frequent exposure to watery tea.

We are a nation of idealists. We are a nation of poets and

we are a nation of conversationalists. We are a nation of die-hards and I will go so far as to say that we are a nation of realists, but we are first and foremost a nation of tea-drinkers, and it could be said that the hand which holds the teapot rules the country. We have our share of coffee drinkers and cocoa drinkers but these are in such a minority that they hardly represent a decent opposition.

There is a traditional and widespread belief that the quality of tea may be judged by whether or not the bottom of the cup is visible to the naked eye. Let me immediately dispel this outrageous fallacy. There are such things as muddy tea and overdrawn tea and, keen as the eye may be, it does not possess the inside knowledge of the long-suffering stomach. Strong tea smells like strong tea. It also looks like strong tea and, most important of all, it tastes like strong tea. Weak tea suffers from pernicious anaemia and the steam from its surface is hardly discernible from its whistling kinsman which hisses from the spout of the common kettle.

During the years ahead, many of our young men will forsake freedom and independence for the more satisfactory and the more consistent joys of matrimony. The principal determining factors by which young men chose their life's companions are in the main governed by wealth, health and general appearance with humour lying a close fourth. These are reliable enough informants and many happy marriages have been made by adhering to such long-established guides. However, a man who accepts a woman on these alone is looking for trouble.

My advice to the young man with an eye to marriage would be to arrange things so that he finds himself in his fiancee's house during tea-time. The procedure should be to sit back calmly answering questions and contributing polite tit-bits to the general conversation. Quietly, and without letting anybody know, he should pay close attention to his cup of tea. If the tea is weak and watery, he should most certainly take stock of his position and ask himself if he is prepared to spend his life in the company of a woman who sees nothing wrong with watery tea. If the tea is strong, he must experience no further doubt. He must marry the girl immediately for there is the danger that word will go out about the potency of her tea, a quality which will enhance her in the eyes of men who are seeking this particular type of girl.

A girl whose people are lovers of strong tea is entitled to the choicest of men. She is safe from ridicule and scorn, and her background is as impeccable as the contents of her mother's tea-caddy.

There is, of course, an infinitesimal section of the country's population, addicted to weak tea. The enlightened man always acknowledges and respects the beliefs of minorities but only while the minority does not seek to impose itself upon the majority. These people must be permitted to drink weak tea as often as they like but they are also duty bound to enquire of their guests if weak tea is acceptable. If not, a second pot of suitable tea must be made immediately. This is not a concession. It is simply an act of common justice.

For a while I myself was subjected to the horrors of weak tea while working abroad. Almost at once two small warts established themselves on the index finger of my left hand. A carbuncle, hitherto-unknown ignominy, appeared on my right arm and the hair on both eyebrows was reduced to a few desolate strands. General debility was the verdict arrived at by the consultant I was forced to visit. Quite by accident I was invited for a cup of tea by a married colleague shortly afterwards. It was strong tea and I drank four cups. The following morning the warts were routed, my eyebrows normal and the carbuncle reduced to the stature of a pimple, and I lived, quite happily ever after.

TWO

SAUCERS OF TEA

Who says it is unmannerly to drink tea out of a saucer?

I am anxious to find out, and I make no bones about it either. I demand the name and address of the person responsible and wish to know from whom he receives his authority – who gives him the right to say: 'You must not drink your tea out of a saucer!'

I refuse to accept his dictatorial admonition and even if I were not in the habit of sometimes pouring tea into my saucer, I would, for the sake of the principles involved, use my saucer in any case; I would use my saucer publicly and without apology just for the sake of finding out the identities of those who endorse this monumental coercion.

All of you who indulge in saucers of tea now and then should band together, should form a society for the protection of your privilege because dictatorship and demagoguery have their roots in injustices of this nature. Do not try to reduce the aggressive content of my question by saying that my questions are not of consequence. Do not dismiss them with a smirk or with the raising of an eyebrow. Instead tell me precisely what is wrong with drinking tea out of a saucer.

There are men, like myself, who dislike overdoses of milk in our tea, men who because of committal to the game of life cannot wait for our tea to cool, men who through no fault of their own are obliged by the indiscriminate candour of circumstance to cool our cups of tea in the shallows of our indispensable saucers. Those who condemn us, who criticize us, and who militate against us, are many. They are the same ones who grin with disapproval when we, spurning the salt-cellar spoon, avail of our more accurately-appointed fingers to take the exact quantity we require and pour the pinch discreetly and without abandon into our eggs, our soups and our porridges or over our fishes, our fowls and our meats. They are the same who chide with ill-mannered cluck-clucks when we use a spoon to grapple with diminutive and elusive peas.

I, personally, have listened to enough comment and read enough criticism belittling the habit of saucer-drinking. It was a practice commended to me by my mother, when, at the age of three, I was entrusted with my own crockery. It is a habit I have found endearing and revealing at hotel breakfast-tables because the use of the saucer is an assurance that one will not be approached by snobs or social climbers. I know that, if a man joins me when my saucer is filled with cooling tea, he is a man in every sense of the word. He is neither a prig nor a proditon. He is a man who knows where he belongs and who believes in staying where he belongs and proves it when he sits at the table of a fellow-traveller who persists in drinking his tea out of a saucer.

I do not drink all my tea out of a saucer. After the first or second saucerful, when the contents of the cup are sufficiently cooled and to show that I am not addicted to discrimination, I drink the remainder of my tea out of my cup. If affected onlookers are disposed towards criticism let me remind them that, for the moment, it is my cup, and it is also my saucer and when I have completed my meal it is I who will have to pay for the use of both.

If my comments to date should be adjudged provocative, I make no apology. The saucer has been misused on repeated occasions and there has been no indignant comment from those who believe themselves to be bolsterers of etiquette. I have seen saucers of snuff at wakes and saucers of ham at wrendances. I have seen borrowed saucers of flour and borrowed saucers of sugar in transit from house to house and I have seen saucers of water in front of electric heaters. I have seen saucers used for purposes which belie their design and tax their resistance and yet no sound of condemnation from the legions of the ethicists. Yet if I, myself, and those who think along the same lines, are forced to pour our tea into our saucers there is an outcry and we are relegated to a class which is not supposed to conform to the high standards prescribed by presentday dietarians.

But, listen to me, you who would scorn and defile us, and listen well, for we are not conscious of the wrongs we have committed and consequently may not take too kindly to your perverse ultimatums.

We will continue, while hot tea continues, and while we feel so inclined, to sit back in our chairs defiantly and fearlessly and enjoy ourselves over the drinking of innumerable saucers of tea.

THREE

INSOMNIA

THERE are several types of insomnia, but they can all be classified under two distinct heads – the kind that keeps you awake, and the kind that won't let you go to sleep.

It cannot be said that one kind is worse than another, since both are unwelcome guests. Insomnia is not an infectious disease, except in the case of husband and wife, when the restlessness of one contributes to the waking of the other.

Too much whiskey has been known to cause insomnia but, on the other hand, in the case of the man who is addicted to his few half-ones before retiring, too little whiskey can cause a pernicious form of insomnia.

Dripping taps have been blamed for much sleeplessness, but whereas you can turn off a dripping tap, you cannot turn off a talkative wife and any attempt to do so is more likely to increase the volume and prolong the flow. A talkative wife is perhaps the greatest single cause of insomnia, although it takes courage to make statements of this nature in public, and while noisy babies are reputed to be a major source, nothing could be further from the truth. In the first place, babies are noisy only for a prescribed period, whereas the talkative spouse is a stayer of far more irritating mettle and while a baby complains because it is hungry the talkative wife is liable to start without provocation of any kind. Indeed a complete absence of provocation is the most powerful stimulant.

Free from the exasperating curse of insomnia are the mothers of large families for the good reason that their sleep is limited to a few short hours and there is little chance that these will be dissipated over the fluctuating gossip of the community. As against this, those who thrive on the plight of neighbours can hardly sleep at all, so great is their impatience for the dawning of another day when they may gloat red-eyed over the most recent disclosures of woe and misfortune.

There is no known cure for insomnia, unless one is willing to accept complete exhaustion but even then sleep can be as elusive as a Stacks' Mountain leprechaun. Sufferers quickly become immune to drugs, draughts and pills, and anyhow these are not to be recommended with impunity. In fact they are not to be recommended at all.

If there is such a thing as the universal cure, pride of place must go to porter, on merit and on merit alone. I am not referring to bottles of porter. I am, of course, referring to pints of porter, it being a well-known fact that three or four pints of porter, judiciously absorbed, have never failed to induce the most blissful of sleeps, the most resolute of sleeps, and the most disinterested of sleeps. The main difficulty with this type of subject lies in trying to keep him awake before he gets into his pyjamas, for he is not above sleeping in his shirt if drowsing impulses are not held at bay. Let it be known, however, that I do not advocate porter freely, nor do I recommend it for novices, with good reason. There are cited cases, where, instead of becoming involved with peaceful slumber, the recipients of excessive doses have been known to burst into song at unearthly hours, thereby contributing to an already high incidence of insomnia.

The disease of insomnia is widespread and has many malignant forms, some of which are not even referred to in the most advanced medical texts. Take, for instance, the acute form sometimes referred to as 'the Rattles' which not only keeps the victim awake but in addition exposes him to the weirdest and most improbable of hallucinations. The root cause of this branch of the insomnia family may be attributed to continued large doses of brandy, gin, rum, whiskey and other lesser-known spirits. This condition is known by many names, the most widely-known being 'the Rats', 'the Willies', 'the Shakes', 'the Clatters', and a variety of other informative titles, the most descriptive of which is, perhaps, 'the Jigs.'

Another strongly-supported cause is the possession of too much money, or the possession of too little as the case may be, since one poses as many problems as the other.

Most people suffer but rarely, and bouts of insomnia are few and far between as far as the man in the street is concerned. The habitual sufferer is a problem, an ever-increasing one in our present-day society. Statistics may not be forthcoming but it is safe to assume that since the advent of income-tax, the number of insomnia victims has trebled.

The question that arises as a result of a recent survey is, whether or not insomnia is likely to become more prevalent. There is every likelihood and every reason to believe that it will. A reduction in the price of the pint would greatly reduce the present number of sufferers, whereas an increase could well send the number rocketing, like the sales of Elvis Presley's records, to unprecedented heights.

The solution, then, lies with the government and it is to be hoped that they will see to it that there will be no upward trend in the devastating disease of insomnia.

FOUR

SHAWLS

'She wore a bonnet, with ribbons on it,
And over her shoulders, she wore a Galway shawl.'
(SONG)

COMING out of Mass last Sunday I counted only one shawl.

The wearer was an old woman. She also wore strong black shoes and thick black stockings and if I was studying her yet I would be hard put to identify her, because shawls, like charity, can cover a multitude.

I remember Masses when more than half of the female worshippers wore shawls. I remarked this to a well-dressed young lady of my acquaintance, who needed the shade of my umbrella on the way out, and her reply was somewhat cold. 'If you paid more attention to the Mass,' she said, 'you wouldn't be bothering yourself with shawls!'

This was the answer I deserved but it was also obvious that the young lady did not approve of shawls. Neither do I approve of shawls, or, strictly speaking, of shawls and nothing but shawls, but shawls have their uses and many a mother in a hurry for last Mass was thankful to snatch a shawl from behind the door, thereby concealing her identity from those who study fashion trends and attiring herself, at the same time, with true humility.

If, on that especial Sunday, the numerous ladies with stiletto heels and pointed toecaps had worn flat shoes like the old lady I mentioned, they would have found little difficulty walking through the slush and snow. Lovers of stiletto heels will, no doubt, disagree, but remember that, with or without them, the shape of a wellmade leg remains the same and that legs were as much admired before stiletto heels as they will be after them.

Progress has almost done away with the common shawl, but progress has given nothing in return, because the shawl was the soul of parity and the essence of equality. I do not blame women who once wore shawls as much as their offspring. Many a hard-working woman was well content with the omniformity of her shawl until her daughters grew up to her and told her the shawl was old-fashioned, without style, and the epitome of poverty. The poor mother had little choice in the face of such strong opposition, and in the end she relented. They bought her a coat which was far too young for her and a hat they wouldn't dream of wearing themselves. I love hats and bonnets of all kinds, but women of the last generation preferred the anonymity of their shawls. The daughters – and in many cases, the sons – did not encourage the transition out of love for the mother. More often than not it happened because they were a-shamed to see their mother wearing a shawl.

I do not say that we should return to shawls altogether. In fact I will sign my name against it if there is a petition, but let us not do away with shawls altogether, and let us not be ashamed of shawls.

I wasn't present at the glittering Irish Derby of last year but I asked a man of my acquaintance if there were any shawls to be seen in that vast and stylish congregation and he assured me that he had not seen one. He saw several thousand fur coats, ranging from beaver to mink and then somewhat hesitantly informed me that there was close on a million pounds worth of new hats and new shoes on view that day 'but,' he said, 'there was no shawl and if I had seen one I'd surely have remembered it.'

The shawl was also a symbol of trust. Nowadays if a man is presented with a vanity purse, containing compact, lip-stick and the rest, it means that he will be seeing the owner home afterwards. Not so long ago a man was put in charge of a certain shawl and if on the way home he proposed to the girl of his choice, no answer was given, but if the shawl was opened so that it covered two instead of one, he knew for a certainty that he had been accepted.

You could carry a baby to Mass under a shawl, and a woman suddenly caught short of bread before supper could throw the shawl over her shoulders without bothering to make-up or change clothes. You could use it for a dressing gown and you can argue the case of smocks as long as you will but the like of it has yet to be invented for expectant mothers. On cold nights it can serve as an extra blanket and on warm days it can be used as a ground rug and where else in the world would a small boy run to escape the wrath of an outraged father.

The shawl is gone, but it is not a question of the shawl having outlived its usefulness. It is a question of our women-folk having outlived the shawl. With the arrival of the motor-car the shawl suffered its greatest single blow but it will never disappear entirely and on Sundays we will continue to see the occasional old woman to remind us of a time when nail-polish was non-existent and the shawl was king.

FIVE

OLD CARS

OLD cars are like old people!

They need to be rested occasionally. They need sympathy and understanding, for great age is often the breeding ground of great bitterness but if a car is looked after with care and love it will grow old gracefully and give as good as it gets.

Recently, I went to Limerick city with a friend of mine. It was a fresh frosty morning as we set out and it was decided that we should travel by the coast road since my friend and I both like a bit of scenery.

The light wind on the Shannon was like a young girl whispering, and my friend whistled happily while we sped over the tree-lined roadway at twentyfive miles an hour.

'She's in good order this morning,' he said, 'and what harm but she has had a hard week of it.'

The doors rattled merrily at this unexpected compliment and from various places in the back came a succession of clanging noises. As we neared Foynes she stopped, for no reason at all.

'That's all right,' my friend said, 'we'll give her a rest till she gets her wind back.'

Ten minutes passed and he started her again. All went well until we reached Askeaton, when our noses were assailed by three distinct burning odours.

'All she wants is a drop of oil,' my friend explained reassuringly. 'We'll have a drop ourselves, too,' he said, 'but a good cowboy always waters his horse first.'

At the petrol pump the attendant looked the car over without change of expression.

'Throw a pint of oil into her,' my friend said.

The attendant returned with a pint of oil, and when the

bottle was empty he shook his head without the least sign of emotion. 'She'd take more than a pint!' he announced.

'She would not!'

'She would!' the attendant said, as if it was none of his business.

'She would, if she got it!' my friend said, and we drove off, a defiant cloud of blue smoke rising behind us. Several uneventful miles passed and finally my friend announced that we were near Limerick.

'How do you make that out?' I asked.

'There's the smoke from the cement factory in front of us.'

'That's not the cement factory,' I said. 'That's the carburettor.'

We pulled up at a labourer's cottage and a small curious man hurried out to inspect us.

'Is she on fire?' he enquired.

'Is there any chance you'd oblige us with a gallon of water?' my friend asked, ignoring the question.

When the gallon was empty, we thanked the kindly cottier who was still regarding our conveyance with a mixture of amusement and ridicule. 'She takes a share of water!' he laughed.

My friend sat behind the wheel again and looked his benefactor straight in the eye. 'If you were after running from Listowel, you might like a sup of water too,' he pointed out.

That night, as we were leaving the city, I was a little apprehensive. My friend sensed my worry. 'You won't hear a word out of her now,' he said; 'she knows we're on the road home.' As we neared home she seemed to grow younger. Now and then she lurched a little to left and right. 'If I gave her her head now,' my friend boasted, 'you wouldn't catch her with a jet, but it wouldn't be fair to her and besides I want her to-morrow.'

'Did you ever think of trading her in?' I asked.

He looked at me with unconcealed astonishment. 'A new car is no good to anyone,' he said defensively. 'It's no good to the garages because it doesn't need repairs, it's no good to the owner because he's afraid he'll tarnish her, and it's no good to a man looking for a lift because new cars are in such a hurry they haven't the time to stop and pick up a person. This ould car gave me the best years of her life. I courted in her, and I proposed in her, and I was accepted in her. I took her on my honeymoon with me and I drove my five children to be christened in her. She never let me down. I know her weaknesses and she knows mine. She knows my pubs and she'll pull up outside them without my having to touch a clutch or a brake. There's no fear she'll be stolen because she'd frighten the life out of a car thief. But I suppose I'll have to get a new car soon, because my sons are growing up to me and there's no one could handle her but myself. But I'd better shut up,' he concluded, 'because all this praise isn't good for her, and she'll probably sulk like a racehorse in the morning.'

SIX

ONIONS

Recently, while passing a shop window, I saw, hanging inside, a string of golden onions.

I passed a month later and there hung the same string, undamaged and unchanged by the passage of time. Surely a remarkable accomplishment for that which is neither fruit nor vegetable. Who but this pungent, edible bulb could improve with age and who is less conscious of its serenity, durability, and dignity? There were bananas, worthy fellows, exhibited on the same window and there were peaches and pears but the thing that caught the eye was the string of onions.

Onion who has flanked and flavoured the proud steak and strengthened its munificent aromas. Onion who has buttressed the frivolous chop enlarging its exuberant vitality. Onion who has ennobled the quivering liver sliver oft mistreated by repeated overturnings. Onion who has feted fecund tripe and sanctified the most sentient of gravies. Onion, with the saliva on my chin, I salute you! I, my friends and my foes, are indebted to you. To you we owe the monumental and relieving belch and the smooth running of the myriad meticulous machinations which occupy our unexplored interiors.

We will not readily forget your right hand in the warring with porter-conscious matrons for you have saved us repeatedly concealing the cataclysmic odour of booze and tempering the malt-laden breath with life-saving camouflage of indigenous versatility. Onion, lowly onion, inured to trial by vegetation. Onion, you have carried mashed potatoes on your back and in bread-stuffing you were the body and soul of the mixture, overpowering stale bread and crusts with indignant whiffs and pauperising parsley with detached superiority. So let it be with stale bread.

Outnumbered in every possible concoction, you have more than held your own, accounted for yourself without bombast or advertisement, and put mightier names to shame when performance was the only criterion.

Wars will be fought but in the end nothing will be resolved and the old injustices ripen as before, but, onion, you were there before them and you will be there after them. Let them make little of you, but you were never governed. No culinary smell dared to usurp you. Onion, prince, oft disparaged by worthless contumely of leek and lettuce and over-awed by burly hearted cabbage – none of them possess your soul. Onion, oft unloved and unestablished still, despite the contribution you have made to countless broths. Onion, oft maligned by lesser entities, in spite of assistance rendered to soups of all sorts, in spite of flavour loaned to unnumbered and uncited stews. In sandwiches, weak apologies for mealtime, you were ever-present. In every trial you stood apart. You were the body and soul of all your allies. You were more! You were yourself, which millions strive to be and, failing, snub you. Onion, cannon of the dispossessed, battlement of the downtrodden, succour of the starving. Fools know you and take you for their own. Kings and emperors adopt you. Flung you were in rage from turrets at the oppressor's head and stripped you were in awful nudity to combat the overpowering smell of paint. Thrust you were into the cavernous bosoms of hanging turkeys and, chopped into scintillating dices, encouraging the poor beef and kidney stew. You have subdued the mighty egg with flavour potent and confounded the back rasher with toothsome deliciousness.

Onion, you are well worth watching and will bear watching always. On sheds of corrugated iron and strung from henhouse doors you have faced the summer heat but yet expiry never neared you. The bestial frosts of harvest were as putty in your hands. The winter winds and rains taunted you in vain. Their worst could not subdue you. The sun you loved above all other, and he, to show his feelings, clothed you in raiment of gold. You shone and bristled in the corded bags of fruiterers. When all fruit fails, then is the onion, and fruit you are in truth and tuber, too. No bough of tended garden tree your likeness ever bore. No pear or peach or plum could match your glowing symmetry. The Irish stew without you is an empty lifeless mess.

Onion, indispensable onion, no housewife dare forget you nor haughty chef has courage to ignore you. Consigned to earthen pit like common fare you did emerge untarnished, glimmering all over like freshly minted gold. Penny, the lowliest of coins, will purchase you. Rare sovereigns will accomplish nothing better. Your breath is as the breath of time. No swirling planet is your peer and yet no poet has taken up his pen to do you justice. Onion, you are the poem and the poet in one, the lyric and the lyricist, the singer and the song. Your monument is your seed.

I hail you and salute you, indefatigable onion!

SEVEN

PLUM-PUDDING

A JOVIAL young fellow of ninety-two frequently calls to see me for no other reason than knowing that he is guaranteed a drop of punch. He assures me that he will live to be a hundred.

Once I asked him to what he owed such a wonderful age.

'I'll tell you,' he said. 'I smoked all the fags and tobacco I could afford, and drank all the whiskey I could lay my hands on. I always stayed up till after midnight and I never did a decent day's work in my life, but I'll tell you what does me real good, and that's a plate of nice plum pudding.'

I agree with him in the last respect for plum pudding is like the globe of the world in more ways than one. First, let there be a glass of dun dark rum from Jamaica and an able-bodied nutmeg from the Malayan Archipelago. Let there be white suet from a portly Irish bullock. Let there be raisins from California and the porous peel of lemons from sun-ridden Cyrenaia. Let there be populous currants from Levant and ginger from the toast flats of the tropics. Let there be cinnamon from far Ceylon and creamy stout from the chuckling Guinness barrels of Dublin.

Apart from all of this, and apart from being a satisfying dessert, plum pudding is also an ideal base for brandy, gin, malt whiskey and bottled stout. It must be steaming hot when served and it must be pampered with several brimming spoonfuls of creamy custard.

The following conversation may be heard any one of these mornings at the grocer's or at the hairdresser's, after Mass, or when babies are being aired along with their mothers in the afternoon:

MAUDE: Great picture at the Oyster last night!

JULIE: Oh! Who was acting in it?

MAUDE: Guess?

JULIE: Let me see now... Cary Grant!... Van Heflin!...

MAUDE: No... my favourites, Gregory Peck and Rock Hudson.

JULIE: Rock Hudson is terrific.

MAUDE: He gets the girl in the end, too. To-night is the last night. She's a nurse and he's a Doctor.

JULIE: Oh, what a shame! The one night I have to stay in!

MAUDE: Gregory Peck takes it well in the end.

JULIE: He's that kind of a man.

MAUDE: You shouldn't miss it. Why don't you make himself stay in?

JULIE: I have to make the plum pudding.

MAUDE: Why don't you buy one in the shop?

JULIE: Do you want me to be murdered? Himself would have a blue fit. He's mad about plum pudding, girl, and he's as cute as a pet fox when it comes to ready-made plum puddings.

The one person who emerges with honours here is the man described as 'himself'. No next-bests for him. He's no Rock Hudson but here, at least, is a man who has set certain standards. Here is a man who is obviously lord and master of his own house. One can visualize, too, a nasty fight in the early years of marriage when, through neglect, she made the disastrous mistake of trying to slip a ready-made pudding across. Not for one moment would I consider consigning such puddings to garbage cans. They are just the job for crusty bachelors who live alone and ideal for those who lack the sense of taste. Let us have ready-made puddings, by all means, but let us have them for ready-made men. Do not feed them to imaginative men who are exhausted from having invented stories about Santa Claus. Do not feed them to men who embraced other men the previous night, who shed tears over the last drink, and who have not forgotten that there were other Christmases when times were not so good and money not so plentiful. Do not place them on the tables of men who remember faraway friends and friends departed for ever, for what good is a pudding that does not lift the heart and what good is a pudding that does not resemble ones shared in other years by another family.

Personally speaking, I like to see my pudding seasoning itself through the weeks which lie ahead of Christmas. I like to see it hanging securely from the ceiling, safe in its mantle of white muslin or airtight flour bag. I like to take my pudding with me to the sitting-room and there sit in front of a roaring fire with the characters I love most around me, then to snooze perhaps and dream, or look into the fire in peace and contentment, there to watch the flames licking the sooty innards of the chimney, particularly if it's cold outside and then perhaps later to be recalled by a familiar voice which says: 'Do you think you'd be able for another slice of plum pudding?'

EIGHT

CONNOISSEURS

A CONNOISSEUR is a well-informed person, competent to pass critical judgment on certain arts and articles, a recognised authority on the finer points of things. The profession is a highly-rated and equally remunerative one and while it may not be as exacting as marathon-running or dyke-scouring, it is an art which contributes in no small way to the peace of the world and in a much greater way to the peace of the home, because the art of keeping one's mouth shut at critical moments is the answer to the unhappy marriage and surely those who are adept at this praiseworthy practice are connoisseurs of the first water.

Every man is a good judge of something. There are people who are excellent judges of seed-cake and rhubarb pies but there is such delicate finesse attached to these specific items that due respect is never attributed to those who make the world a better place because of the high standards they demand. Some people are authorities on turnip-seed but at the same time utterly ignorant of the volumes of hydrogen peroxide and its effects on the female head. Others are experts on the quality of quarter-tips and half-soles and could tell you, from the smell of the leather or the space between the tacks, whether or not the shoemaker was proficient at his trade.

We hear of a man being a good judge of a woman. This is not to say that he will judge her points as he would a filly's, but rather that he knows to a nicety the type of woman best suited to him. A man of five foot four would look out of place with a girl of six feet and a man of eight stone must not be expected to hold his own with a girl of fifteen.

Woe betide a man who is not a connoisseur in matters of

the heart. You can always sell a horse or swap a pony but, for better or worse, the woman of the house is a permanent installation. Connoisseuring, as certain affected quarters would have us believe, is not confined to the criticism and classification of paintings or sculpture. Indeed there is a far greater art in knowing exactly how much salt to put in one's soup without tasting first. Fortunes have been made by men who were authorities on fat bullocks and men have achieved immortality from being good judges of seed potatoes. How many times have we heard in public-houses: 'The Lord have mercy on him, but he was a powerful judge of oats!'

Everyman is a connoisseur in his own right and while it may be more profitable and fashionable to pronounce upon obscurity, the man who knows that corned beef does not agree with him is better paid in the long run. The artist who can keep gastritis continually at bay has, in the words of the theatre critic, arrived.

There are men who can smell trouble miles away but who have the happy knack also of being at another situation when it arrives. Old men with watery eyes and wrinkled cheeks can smell rain in the wind, or know by the antics of a tom-cat when thunder will be heard. Old women are informed by creaky joints about the arrival of sleet, and canny pensioners know by the tingling at the butts of their ears that journeys should be postponed because frost is heralded. I once knew a man who put on his new clothes and shaved himself whenever his left leg became itchy. He then journeyed to town where he collected a registered letter in the post office. All these, however, are feelings which are commonplace enough. The dedicated connoisseur is fast disappearing from the scene.

There was a time, not so long ago, when certain public-houses maintained their own connoisseurs, but that was during the era of the wooden barrels. Men of this particular denomination were only to be found in bars where the licensee was a widow, or the proprietor a believer in total abstinence. When a barrel was tapped, a half-pint of the new porter was placed on the counter. The connoisseur first smelled it and, after a prescribed period, raised it to his lips. A tiny sip to begin with and suddenly, with a fabulous swallow, the glass was drained. If he nodded his head, all was well, but if he frowned the barrel was taken off and a new one tapped in its stead. His presence was vital to communities where men were finicky about their porter. If a customer maintained that his pint was casky, the connoisseur was called upon to decide the issue, and a pint of the doubtful vintage poured. It goes without saying, of course, that the drink was paid for by the man who made the complaint. The expert swallowed the draught and rolled his eyes around in frightening deliberation. He screwed his chin under his upper lip and wrinkled his forehead. There was a doubt! The issue hung in the balance and another pint was called for by interested parties who fancied themselves as judges of porter. The pint was duly swallowed and a verdict awaited. The connoisseur grinned, but he also smiled. Impossible to form an opinion without supporting evidence. Another pint and yet another until at last he indicated by a resounding belch that he was prepared to pronounce judgment. Silence in court! With a full belly and the strut of satiety, the connoisseur staggered towards the door, concluding as he did so that no porter was bad but that some was better than more.

NINE

SPARE-RIBS

THERE are many ways of creating an embarrassing situation.

You can yell at the top of your voice at the height of a solo performance in a concert hall, or you can arrive at an exclusive wedding reception wearing morning suit and brown shoes. You can sing in court, or obscure a man's view during a football final but those are quickly forgotten and the memory diminishes with the passage of time.

There is only one sure way to cause unequivocal upheaval and that is to walk into a Grade A hotel at the height of the tourist season and ask for boiled spare-ribs and turnips for your dinner.

The first thing the waiter will bestow upon you is an indulgent smile but when you repeat the request you will notice a slight change on his smug features, a mixture of revulsion and annoyance, calculated to put you in your place and readymade for such occasions, to show you that you are in the wrong hotel. It calls for a man of strong convictions to repeat the request the third time. If you are a member of a party, the waiter has the advantage because he thrives on the embarrassment of uncertain guests who will accept anything rather than be involved in a scene but if a man is alone and courageous he will not be cowed, particularly if his background is of consequence.

Lest I be misunderstood in this matter, let me define the word background. A man with background is one who is not ashamed of the fact that he prefers porter to absinthe. He is a man who feels naturally out of place with a coffee cup which might have come from a doll's set. He is a man who is proud of the table which fed him from infancy and who doesn't give a tinker's curse about the opinions of

waiters regardless of intimidation and affected superiority.
He is a man who knows the particular idiosyncracies of his
own stomach, because, after all, it is his stomach and not
the waiter's which will have to digest the fare for which he
pays. He is a man who wears ordinary trousers when all
around him are wearing narrow ones and, most important
of all, he is a man who would be equally at home at a cocktail party or swallowing cold bacon and hot tea at the shady
corner of a meadow. He is a man who can do without
poodle-dogs and after-shave lotions if he has to, but he is a
man who cannot do without an occasional feed of spare-
ribs.

The meat on a spare-rib is as succulent as lobster, tender
as chicken and sweet as mountain honey. The meat on a
spare-rib, boiled or roast, is among the most delicate yet
satisfying of all the innumerable dishes which have graced
the tables of mankind since the first wild pig wallowed in the
muds of antiquity, and it should therefore be remembered
that it is not among the capital sins to expect an occasional
reminder of its presence on the menus of our more exclusive
hotels.

We have all but sold our stomachs to the French and
aped their fanciful concoctions for too long. All the foods in
France thrown together lose face in the presence of spare-
ribs if a man has a mind for them. Very good if you are
inclined towards the French way, I will not intrude upon
your affectations, but neither will you intrude upon mine
because I am prepared to go to any length to defend the
spare-rib. I will continue to ask for them in hotels and
maybe managements one day will realise that spare-ribs are
no less respectable than chicken saute marengo or coq au
vin.

In the Old Testament sparrows were common provender. Don't ask me whether they stuffed or boiled them but
if ordinary sparrows were good enough for the bearded

patriarchs of yesterday, surely spare-ribs are good enough for us. I have it, in the strictest confidence, from an elderly lady, whose name I cannot reveal, that never once during the ninety seven years of her stay in this world did she suffer from any sort of stomach disorder. When asked by a visiting journalist to what she owed her longevity, she answered 'spare-ribs', surely proof enough to convince the most adamantine diehards that there are other things in life beside Spaghetti Bolognese and butterscotch tapioca.

There is a question which may be safely deleted from the starchy dialogue of waiters if spare-ribs ever appear on menus, and that is: 'What will you have to follow, sir?' because nothing dare follow a well-presented spare-rib. Anything else would be superfluous and tell me, who would want chocolate fudge on top of boiled cabbage, floury potatoes and spare-ribs?

TEN

THE MUG

You must go back a few years first, and come with me to a certain eating-house where men who scour dykes and plough fields foregather. There weren't any chairs and there were no flowers, but there were long, low forms and brightly scrubbed tables.

There were bustling efficient women with spotless white aprons and faces wreathed with morning smiles. You could call for half a loaf of bread and a mug of soup and you left the place as full as if you had eaten four fourcourse dinners.

You faced the road home with the heat of true substance glowing inside of you and you didn't suffer from gastritis or flatulence either, because the simpler the fare the better the reception from quarters which can be difficult.

There was soup in those days, soup with body in it and thick enough to march a battalion of mice across its surface. There were mugs in those days, real mugs with patterns of highland scenery where gentle does dallied with lovable fawns and stags stood defiantly on crags of unbelieveable beauty.

You could hardly blame a gullible young country lad for believing that those selfsame mugs had no bottoms to them because it was when you thought the soup was nearly gone that the real surprises were in store for you.

The bottom of the mug was a revelation, for here you might find chopped onions and occasional green peas, diced carrots and sliced turnips and maybe a morsel of chicken's liver or a piece of boiling beef that would dissolve like jelly in your mouth if you tried to chew it.

A man who has risen from his warm bed at all hours of the morning will know what I am talking about and I bet he'll shake his head fondly, remembering cold bitter dawns of long ago and contrary cattle that often broke a man's heart when they took off without rhyme or reason for unknown pastures in the depths of mysterious bogs where the pursuer often found himself up to his knees in ice-cold water.

He will remember hands that were blue with cold and noses that nearly fell off from the stinging swipes of an east wind. He won't readily forget the long hours spent standing in an open street when money was scarce, and bluff, hardhearted jobbers were only too eager to take advantage of a man whose rates were long overdue and whose flour bin was nearly empty.

Maybe these things are forgotten because times are better and money is more plentiful, but there is a moment he will never forget and that is the glorious instant when he curled cold fingers around a hot mug filled to the brim with soup that made itself felt the second its odour assailed a famished nostril.

A cup wasn't much use to a man who had ten miles put behind him over mountainy roads. It was dwarfed by his calloused hands and it was only when he had a mug in his grasp that he felt the security and comfort due to a man who has earned his rates and met his obligations.

Mugs are not confined to soup by any means because there were tea-mugs and grog-mugs and the mug for the ould women's nightly dose of salts, and there were mugs which were pressed on rolled dough if you wanted to bake a pan of circular buns.

There were mugs that were used for borrowing sugar, and mugs that measured periwinkles and cockles, and larger mugs used in the selling of gooseberries and early onions.

It surprises me that in a world where great wars were fought over ephemeral oddities such as national boundaries, that conflict or civil strife was never instituted by a mug. I have heard of houses where tempers glowed white hot as a result of a man taking the wrong mug for his supper.

The first defensive blows struck by the toddler were occasioned when his mug was in danger of being purloined, and his first glimpses of art were prints of pompous goosey-ganders and scraggly-haired witches on brooms.

A mug, too, was the symbol of authority and was used only by the man who sat at the head of the table. I'll grant you that the baby of the house had his mug but his status was no more than that of a court jester. The true symbol of authority was the large plain mug of the male parent and sacrilege hardly fitted the magnitude of the sin when it was broken.

The guilty party trembled with fear while judgement was awaited. It was useless to try and replace the broken article because the moment the master of the table took his first deliberate mouthful he knew by the taste of his tea that fraud had been perpetrated.

There was little flippancy about men who drank their tea out of mugs. There was a solidity about them that ensured dry turf for the long winters. A small boy could not help but feel secure when he sat at the opposite end of a table from a man who wore an open shirt with the sleeves rolled up, who could beckon with the barest flicker of an eyelid when the time had come for someone to sit on his lap and maybe sup strong tea from the cherished mug in preparation for the day when he himself would Rave a mug of his own.

ELEVEN

AFTER THE PLAY

THE playwright stood defiantly on the stage and listened with contempt to the howls of a disappointed audience. He held his head high and in his eyes was the long-suffering look of the truly great artist. Try as he might, he could not make himself heard above the boos of the crowd. Unexpectedly, a head of rotten cabbage came soaring over the heads of the audience from the end of the hall. It struck the author fairly and squarely on the nose and put him sitting on his behind. Loud laughter followed, and derisive yells rose everywhere. Then there was a strange quiet. Rising, the author picked the head of cabbage from the boards and looked at it sadly. In a low voice he said: 'Somebody has lost his head. I'd better leave before you all do.' He exited with considerable dignity.

When an author faces the public after the presentation of one of his own plays, he is placed in an extremely difficult position. Entering from the wings, he smiles weakly at the assembled cast as if they were complete strangers to him. They return the smile fearfully and turn towards the audience apologetically, thereby giving the impression that they are not prepared to be associated in any respect with the subsequent revelations of a man who, as everybody knows, is utterly irresponsible.

Some of the more thirsty members of the company breathe silent but fervent aspirations, hoping for a mercifully brief speech. Under the new licensing laws, every minute counts and the longer the address lasts the more murderous the expressions on the faces of those who are not used to doing without a few pints at night. The terrible realization dawns on them as the flow goes on that the author himself is well-primed for the occasion and doesn't give a tinker's curse for the misfortunes of others.

The secret of the successful first night is to speak shyly, haltingly, apologetically, and, above all, disparagingly about the play in question. Throw in the odd joke but never give the audience time to think. Ply them with regretful reminders of the play's failings and look downcast and sheepish as if you were thoroughly ashamed of yourself. It is not a good idea to appear on stage with a baby in one's arms but crutches may be used legitimately, or, if this seems like overdoing it, a successful ruse is not to shave for a week beforehand and to climb on to the stage assisted by friends. Nobody will jeer at a sick man. However, the safest bet is the apologetic tone, the air of perfect humility, the dejected appearance. People will leave the hall, saying: 'Well, now, wasn't he a very unassuming fellow, so natural. Sure, you'd think he never wrote a play at all.' The fact is that he never did but he has cunningly gained a brief respite until the morning papers catch him out. It is no harm to point out that if this procedure is exaggerated, there can be disastrous results.

There is the classic example of the too-modest playwright who received his just deserts for laying it on a bit too thickly. On the first night he appeared on the stage with a devout expression on his face. He had the appearance of a man who has been interrupted in the middle of his prayers. He looked soulfully and piously at his audience and started his address. 'Ladies and gentlemen,' he began, 'if there is any credit due for the writing of this play, it is due to God, not to me. So thank God instead of me.' Religiously he stood his ground while the audience applauded hysterically. Suddenly an old woman jumped to her feet and shouted: 'Ah! the blackhearted blackguard! He won't even take the blame himself!'

Most first-night audiences respond well to a play regardless of its quality. If the hall is small, the clapping goes on and on, because the author's relations far outnumber the regular theatregoers. If the theatre is large and fashionable, the patrons come, not to look at a play, but to have a look at one another. They shout: 'Autah! Autah!' This is not done because of any desire to see the unfortunate man who wrote the play but because everybody else is shouting and no one wants to look odd. Anyhow, they are almost invariably disappointed in what they see. If the author has taken one too many, he is dissipated. If he is badly dressed, he is depraved and if he is sober and respectable-looking, he is stuck-up. Some authors insult their audiences and while this may be alright for society folk who don't know whether or which, it could quite easily finish up with an assault from those who take themselves too seriously. There is no real harm in this either because the ensuing publicity has the same commercial value as a rave review. Shaw once stepped on the stage after a premiere, to be greeted with rapturous applause from a delighted audience. When the clapping had expired, a man rose in the gallery, and booed for all he was worth. 'I agree with you, sir,' Shaw thundered, 'but who are we two against so many?'

A sensible approach to the question of first-night addresses would be to harangue the audience in Londonderry Irish, a solution which on the one hand would send the audience home as ignorant about the author as when they arrived and on the other hand create the impression that he was a man dedicated to home, faith and fatherland.

TWELVE

ON PANDY

Let porter fresh from laughing barrels
Abolish life's unending quarrels;
And if there's plates and saucers handy
Fill up the lot with steaming pandy.

(ANONYMOUS)

THE unknown balladmaker who put these lines together will not be remembered for his contribution to the annals of great poetry, but he will be remembered with some pride and affection by men who liked pandy. He will be quoted by moist-eyed men who are not ashamed of their backgrounds. I have nothing personal against the use of bread-stuffing in roast fowls. Each to his own taste. Let there be no bitterness or misunderstanding. I am only doing what must be done.

I want merely, from a feeling of national conscience, to denude bread-stuffing of much of its grandeur and glamour and give it the status it deserves. Surely nothing could be fairer than that and, after all, what is bread-stuffing but the transformation of stale bread into an unattractive mass, acceptable to those who do not know any better. It is fraudulent. I am not being deliberately provocative or endeavouring to stir up controversy but I have strong feelings about this particular subject. It was the harbinger of rock-'n'-roll, the atom bomb and the bikini. To the truly fastidious, it is totally unacceptable. To the now almost extinct species of open-hearted or convivial Irish gourmand, it will never usurp potato-stuffing. I should, of course, have said 'Pandy' but in these days of diced potatoes there is a certain weariness in expressing natural sentiments publicly.

'Pandy', the only bisyllabic word likely to replace the

infantine 'da-da'; pandy – like the deliciously-sentimental songs of Foster – is threatened by the ephemeral fads of to-day. Let those who want mashed potatoes have mashed potatoes, but I will not condone a dry, white mass, devoid of onions, milk and butter. What good is bread-stuffing to hands that are calloused by plough-handles, or to men who work in offices all day.

Things have come to a terrible pass. It is no longer wise in certain societies to express longing for a grilled red-herring. The mention of black puddings and home-made drisheens is taboo. Even periwinkles are frowned upon. What I would like to ask is – who is to blame? It is a matter that I would like to take up with those responsible. If the word 'pandy' is mentioned, it is done in whispers by kind-faced middle-aged men who remember with moist eyes a mother's cry from yesterday: 'Your pandy is on the table, dear; come in before 'tis cold!'

I am not campaigning for a return to the old ways. Much of what is new is good. All I ask for is a minor concession. I appeal to the young housewife. There is no greater joy than chasing a small boy who has absconded with a fistful of exposed pandy from the goose she is basting.

How many are left who remember the great delights of yesterday? I would like to know the man who is not moved at the sight of steaming handy I will throw caution to the winds and go further. I would like to meet him personally and hear him out to the end of his prejudice. I am not a fighting man, but I will not be pushed.

One thing leads to another. Bread-stuffing leads to a wine-list. A wine-list calls for knowledge, which is the least; also considerable cash, which is the most. Pandy does not need to be buttressed. Like the lighthouse, it stands alone.

I am not wholly blaming this new generation for the threat to Pandy. The portents were evident a long time ago. The Egyptians, the Greeks, the Romans and the Irish held that fair warning was always given before the advent of decline. Warning in this case was given, unless I am greatly mistaken, when began the inconsiderate placing of forks to the left of a person and knives to the right. The lefthanded man was not considered here. This was the first threat to the individual; the first instance of a similar treatment for the masses. Here the human spirit must rebel. We have been pushed far enough. A stand must be made somewhere. The black pudding has been reduced to garbage level. The red herring has been consigned to the night-watchman. Pandy will shortly be associated with a certain trade or profession. It may be yours! If we are to make a stand, what nobler one than in defence of pandy.

THIRTEEN

SALUTING PEOPLE

SALUTING people is tricky and troublesome.

It is unavoidable, necessary, overdone and underdone, and an art which few have thought it worth while to cultivate.

I knew a man once who refused to acknowledge the salutes of his neighbours for thirty seven years. Nobody could explain his churlishness and lack of courtesy until one day towards the end of his life he appeared wearing a pair of hornrimmed spectacles with exceedingly strong lenses. These succeeded in completely changing his manners and turning him into the most considerate and obliging of men. He was a ledger clerk and until the purchase of the glasses could hardly see three feet in front of him. On one occasion he was struck on the right ear which resulted in his having to spend five days in bed. An angry neighbour on his way home from a wedding breakfast had wished him the time of day and, receiving no reply, had committed the aforesaid act. But for the intervention of a plucky messenger boy, there is no telling where the assault might have ended.

On the same street there lived another whose behaviour was held to be unaccountable. One day he would respond cheerfully to the salute of a neighbour. The next day he would not. People said he was odd and one old woman, who was renowned for the conclusions she made from secret observations of people, said he was a head case and should not be let loose among civilized people. The result was that people slammed their doors in his face whenever he felt obliged to make a social call. He was overlooked upon the occasions of neighbourhood parties and although a keen supporter of steeplechasing was never once asked to take a seat in a car to Killarney Races or elsewhere. Eventually he moved away to a new locality. There his asthma disappeared, his assistance was always on offer, and he was consulted frequently about such irrelevant matters as teething problems and the suitability of bedside lamps. He became godfather to nineteen children and when he died the street was blocked by the number of motorcars at his funeral.

Saluting people is a fad. Some cannot live without it while others consider it a nuisance. There is never a guarantee that the person to whom the salute is given will return it. On the other hand, if no salute is proffered there is always the offchance that a person renowned for never saluting will make this an occasion for doing so. So what is one to do? At best saluting people is a necessary evil. It is harder than sending Christmas cards, for whereas Christmas comes but once a year, people you know by sight are encountered every day. How many women rush home in high dudgeon with the following complaint for the ears of a drowsy husband: 'I saluted that so-and-so down the road and she didn't even look at me!' Of course she didn't look at her for the good reason that she had something else on her mind. Maybe a demand note for Rates had come in the morning's post or maybe her daughter was talking of getting married to a known waster or, worse still, maybe she was after discovering that her husband didn't love her anymore. If you are in the habit of saluting a person and if the person misses out now and then, what are a few forgotten salutes in a lifetime? I will concede, however, that there are people who deliberately shun others because of the difference in their social stations, but these people are to be pitied, not blamed. There are people who deliberately ignore a salute because they have been told that the person in question said something about them. These are natural enough failings and people are to be forgiven for such paltry emotions but the person who calculates a snub to a nicety deserves a boot in the behind because some people are easily hurt and cannot be expected to know that it is more important to have the goodwill of the majority than the ostracism of the few.

Saluting people is like chain reaction. A certain king will snub a certain duke, a certain duke will snub a certain earl, until we have a certain tuppence-ha'penny snubbing a certain tuppence. Human beings are invested with many failings but deliberate misuse of the power to salute is one of the most contemptible. Some people suffer from embarrassment and may light a cigarette or bend to tie a bootlace until the party has passed. I have known men to duck behind doorways or sneak into publichouses to escape an embarrassing encounter. Others stop at shop windows and scrutinize advertisements as if their lives depended on it. This attitude may result from shyness, perversity, ignorance or downright stupidity.

The best plan is to salute everybody. It costs nothing and if people don't salute back, it is not the end of the world. You never know when a man is contemplating the assassination of an Income Tax assessor or upset because he has had a tiff with his missus. So to-morrow if I don't salute you on the street, you'll understand, won't you, and if you don't salute me I'll do my best to understand, too. But, for heaven's sake, the next time the woman down the street fails to salute you, don't make an issue out of it because I have it on good authority that her husband is worried about losing his job; her son in England hasn't written home for six months, and she is at the age herself when women do not feel so good, so I think you'll agree that she'll be her old saluting self again when things brighten and fortune smiles a little on her unhappy existence.

FOURTEEN

GRAVY

> '*I love the sea, I love the navy,*
> *I like my biscuits dipped in gravy.*'
> (SONG)

THERE never has been, and as far as I can make out, there never will be a proper appreciation of gravy.

If you ask a waitress in an hotel for a drop of gravy she will look at you as if you were a two-headed man, while you may be sure that she would never dream of sitting down to her own dinner without a few spoonfuls to soften the meat or wet the potatoes. One cannot be blamed for believing that waiters and waitresses keep it all for themselves. This may be totally untrue but sometimes it is very hard on a man who has been reared on gravy and who still fervently believes that gravy is as important as the meat from which it derives many of its basic attributes.

In the house where I was reared, spoonfuls or 'greasings' of gravy were considered to be laughing matters, and it was thought dangerous to insult a man by pestering his meat with such minute quantities. A large jug, containing an approximate quart of rich, brown, steaming gravy was placed upon the table's centre, and if that wasn't enough more was processed immediately by mysterious means, unquestioned means and, above all, acceptable means. The beauty about the 'second run' as I will call it is that it bore no resemblance in either appearance or taste to the first. This is not to say that it fell behind in quality, because what it lacked in meat content it more than made up for in the imaginative and incomparable composition of a mother who knew to a nicety that which would encompass the peculiar tastes of all. No mean art this, but an accepted one, since it is commonplace.

The tastiest gravy I ever ate was made with the conniv-
ance of roast veal. People do not eat quarters of veal any
more. One of the reasons is that calves are too dear but
even when calves were plentiful and sold at seven-and-six
per head there were people who could not or would not
stomach veal. The truth is that they weren't hungry enough
because there is no just reason, allergy apart, for disliking
veal. But about this particular gravy. The quarter of veal
was butchered and the various joints, well dusted with
flour, were placed in a pan where bacon lard had been at
work for some while previously. Needless to mention there
must have been some correspondence beforehand between
veal and lard because as soon as they met, both burst into
song and while the ensuing cacophony might not have
satisfied the conductors of symphony orchestras, it boded
well for those who had partaken of light breakfasts.

Sparkling ballerinas of hot fat high-stepped it in the air
while at ground level a chorus of chuckling bubbles sere-
naded the cooking veal. Later when the chorus had died to
a throaty gurgle of satisfaction, the veal was taken from the
pan and placed in a large dish until the gravy was ready.

A specially-chosen onion was then peeled and reduced to
slices which did not exceed one-third of an inch in thickness. A fistful of flour was creamed into a cupful of water
and added slowly but surely until the required thickness
was achieved. A little colouring concluded the contributions
of supporting interests. The mixture was then allowed to
simmer for several minutes and the final result was a brown
gravy of such exquisite quality that couriers were frequently
despatched to neighbouring houses to enquire if there were
any potatoes left over after the dinner. It must be said,
however, that the main credit for this type of gravy goes to
the bacon lard.

Sauces out of bottles are acceptable nowadays to most

palates but this again is further proof of the low standards of to-day. A dinner without gravy, like faith without good works, is dead, and unless I am mistaken spasms, colic and gripe are unknown to households where gravy is consumed in quantity. Furthermore, I have always found respect, obedience and courtesy in youngsters who came from homes where there is no scarcity of gravy and in future when I am obliged to dine in an hotel I am going to insist upon my rights. I am not going to sit silent if presumptuous moisture plays the role of pretender. I will be polite, but firm. I will not be demanding, but neither will I be apologetic, because the Constitution has given the citizen certain rights. I am going to ask for gravy and if I do not get it I am going to repeat my request. If I still do not succeed in getting what I want, I will straighten my tie, blow my nose, muster what little dignity I possess and walk out the door of that hotel, not in annoyance, mark you, but with renewed grit and determination to continue with my search until I find a place at last where there is no shortage of gravy.

FIFTEEN

DUCKEGGS

SCIENCE has carried man far, and dissolved as many mists as a sou'wester, yet in the nicer mysteries of man's innate make-up, duckeggs have played the greater role. Man has learned much over the recent decades but in the ultimate analysis when the great truths will be laid bare, it will be discovered that he has forgotten more.

The successful piloting of a jet-plane is achievement of a high order, but give me the man who can put a small teat on an eight-ounce baby bottle in total darkness when panic is rife all around him and he can depend on no one to come to his aid, and while a satellite whirling in its proportionately infinitesimal orbit is awe-inspiring, it cannot compare with the fresh beauty of a bobbing rectangle of boiled duckeggs on a kitchen table at dawn.

When our ancestors foregathered for the great trip to Clontarf they made the journey without tinned beef or sausage-rolls in their haversacks. Their strength was the terrible strength of men who were reared on duckeggs and their anger was implacable against the herring-fed hosts of the foe.

Sadly enough, however, the era of duckeggs is disappearing. They are now relegated to the awful chemistry of porter-cakes, whipped into dishonourable disunity, made to congregate with irresponsible currants, and, without regard for rank or principle, expected to mix with capricious spices, sombre almonds and gaudy cherries, oddities that have never been regarded as stable diets by men of respectability and substance.

Of late, we have grown proud and intolerant from affected discernment. We are inclined to look down our noses at the dishes of our fathers, and it is chilling to think that a rising generation is in danger of going through life without being able to distinguish between hen-eggs and duck-eggs.

Fastidiousness is a commendable trait, but it can be carried too far, and in extremity can threaten an old but superior order of things; can, in short, if applied repeatedly, put a man off his duckeggs and leave him with a feeling of frustration and shame.

A word of warning may not be amiss before I go further. Duckeggs are not for the uninitiated or the immature. You cannot confront a growing boy with a brace of duckeggs and expect him to relish them without the due process of apprenticeship, but the toddler who has experimented with the caps laid aside for that express purpose by a far-sighted father will grow up with a love for foods that have weathered the tastes of centuries, and you may be sure that his eggshells will be empty when his spoon is put aside and his feet are stretched indolently on the kitchen floor.

We are told that these are days of hygiene and sanitation, but people would seem to be ignorant of the fact that the duckegg has been on the market since the first squawk was heard by a riverside, untouched by hand or machinery, and sealed by a process without parallel in the long and boastful annals of science and mechanization.

To be sure, the tin has its advantages, but there is a deeper meaning and a more profound feeling of security when a man returns from out-of-doors at daybreak with a capful of duckeggs for the breakfast of his flock, safe in the knowledge that his ducks will not betray him should calamity befall the economics that would govern him.

Strangely enough, there are people of unimpeachable background and reportedly mature outlook who, by wanton and inconsiderate actions, have subjected the innocent duckegg to undeserved ridicule and invested it with characteristics which belong to the fauces of creation.

Why will educators persist in drawing the outline of a duckegg under the compositions of dunces? Why not a straight line, or a cross, or, if they have undisciplined artistic tendencies, what would be wrong with the young of the species of the porcupine? Why do sportsmen say duck, instead of nil, thereby attaching an unwarranted stigma where it least belongs? Sportsmen, indeed! Better far to say nothing if you cannot say something good.

It is disheartening to think that men will tackle the pony no more after a Sunday dinner and ready the trap for one of those great expeditions into the hinterlands of a faraway parish where dwelt a certain woman who kept a good clutch of eggs. No money exchanged hands, for it was a matter of common courtesy to spread the good seed far and wide. There was the reward from hearing in after years of a handsome drake at the other side of the mountains who had made his mark in life and not disgraced the honourable clutch from which he came.

It would be churlish of me to belittle the great fame of hen-eggs and futile to detract from their importance in the everyday pattern of things that are with us. There is too much discord in the world for the good of order and peace, but surely we are not going to stand for further delineation of a cherished dish, a food beloved by our ancestors? If we are to be deprived of the duckegg, other more valuable commodities will follow in short order, and once the rot sets in there is no telling where it will stop.

I am not saying that civilization as we know it must come to an end, but it never does harm to be prepared, and a man with a couple of duckeggs under his belt has the equipment to cope with whatever a changing world has to offer him and the sustenance to endure the challenges of tomorrow.

SIXTEEN

ONION DIP

DEVOTEES of seed cake, sausage rolls and salad cream are not, I am happy to say, among my close friends. I will not be hanged for detraction or calumny when friedbread fanatics are under discussion. I will take my chance and have a drink with the man who raves over boiled rhubarb, but I may tell you this from my heart out, I will not be seen crying at any of their funerals.

Additionally, at the risk of making enemies, I am prepared to state that frivolities of the kind I have mentioned are responsible for more ulcers than one income tax assessment notice and two bank overdrafts, and I will bet a six-inch nail to a tack that if a Gallup poll is made you will find that there is no incidence whatsoever of ulceration where the subjects are people who are fortified by onion dip.

Plaice, properly filleted, sole on the bone, and spring salmon are remarkable fish – fish whose families were well-to-do when Yorkshire sauces were unnecessary – but, somehow, I feel that they, too, have their limitations.

On the other hand, onion dip is a noble and conscientious diet, notable chiefly for its lack of grandiose illusions, but with the happy knack of making friends easily with the most intractable and garrulous of digestive organs.

No ode of consequence has been composed to the onion and few artists have sought inspiration from its golden vested glowing rotundity, but then most artists are habitues of fish-and-chip shops and are more intimate with ordinary sausages who shriek and scream like stuck pigs the moment the first spatter of aggressive fat scalds their sickly coverage. It is no wonder that modern artists cannot paint. Is there an artist of the modern trend breathing who can paint a signpost which every motorist will understand?

God be with the time when a man was judged by the amount of turf he cut in the round of a day, and God be with the day when a man might make a name for himself on the strength of the number of potatoes he ate for his dinner, when, without chop, liver or rind, but on the strength of dip alone he could thin more turnips and mow more hay than any nowadays herd of dripping-fed Teddy-boys.

But a man should not be judged because of his preferences. There is no real harm in the occasional sausage and one must make allowance if men get unusual notions occasionally. Frequently, after a feed of plain porter, a man's mind will turn to chips, and if he is seen staggering down a poorly-lighted laneway with a bag in his hand, one should forgive rather than condemn, because, after all, each of us has his weakness and it is unwise to judge without deified portfolio. A line must be drawn somewhere, however, and it is here that onion dip comes into its own.

There are one hundred and twenty two ways of making onion dip, but there are only four ingredients involved in the requisite formula – the onion, the milk, the flour and the butter. Even at this present time, when a moderate meal can cost a man 10/- and what is described as full dinner an even pound, a growing family of ten can be fed adequately and completely at a total cost of 8/-. The labour involved is incidental, since it is granted freely by a mother who would not be otherwise engaged. There are no assistant chefs because she likes to attend to these small chores herself. All that is required is a stone of spuds, a pound of onions, a few ounces of flour, and a half-pound of butter.

The onions, of course, must be like good corner-forwards, small and knacky but solid and compact when the heat is on. It will be suggested by unprincipled delineators that onion dip is not sustaining, that onion dip is not nourishing, that onion dip is a peasant dish unfit for the chaste palates of gentlemanly fellows who are the Honourable so-and-so's by title but no better than the rest of us by nature... Onion dip is a staunch, strengthening mixture and a plate of it, aided and abetted by honest potatoes, a handy knob of butter and a few dusteens of pepper and salt, is a more appetising presentation than the most vaunted excuse for a dinner that ever came out of a graded eatin' house in the hygienic city of London.

There is no name for onion dip as a meal in the language of the French, because as smart as the French were our grandmothers were a damn sight smarter and while snails and molluscs may have made strong contribution to the fodder of the Breton, you wouldn't scour many dykes or de-horn many bullocks if you had to depend on them.

I once knew a man who composed 600 lines of composite iambic pentameter to the barnacle goose and was thereafter a martyr to heartburn. If he had used his wits as competently as his pen, he might have had the good sense to indulge once in a while in onion dip and his widow would not now be plagued by an assortment of congenital idiots, who, in all probability, despised her late husband's compositions.

When all food fails and men are weakening for unknown reasons and drinking to rid themselves of trouble, a sauce-pan of onion dip on the cooker and a few freshly boiled spuds often put a man back on the road to sobriety, confused his enemies, and reminded him of the great simplicity that a contented stomach makes for a contented home.

SEVENTEEN

'SCENES'

*The love of man for woman waxeth and
waneth as the moon, but the love of
brother for brother is constant and
endureth even as the rolling of the sea.*

(FROM THE ARABIC)

I DO NOT agree with the latter-end of this excerpt, for brothers can be the most vicious foes of all, but the first part is true because love has its ups and downs and those who fully appreciate it will experience true happiness.

It is no good to say that scenes should be avoided, because scenes, like evil, must be met head on and I think it is true to say that the man and woman who appreciate and acknowledge each other's weaknesses will rise above the occasion to a better understanding of each other.

When I hear of the married couple who never had a scene, I am reminded of the just man who instead of falling seven times a day had the incredible fortitude never once even to stumble. Scenes and rows, provided they are limited to two participants, are good for the constitution. Doubts are dispelled in the process and suspicions disposed of. Faults and failings are exaggerated and libellous accusations thrown wildly about but a scene between two people who are fond of each other is as purifying as a snow-laden wind and, more important by far, than spring cleaning and if, by chance, you ever meet a man who tells you that he never had a tiff with his missus be sure to shake his hand and sympathise with him because, as sure as there are vitamins in periwinkles, this man is the product of a disastrous marriage.

I remember an old tinker-man, whose wife had passed

on, who, when asked if he missed her much, replied: '"Tis heartbreakin!" I have no one now to fight with!' Many a marriage was saved from its greatest foe, complacency, by the airing of grievances and mutual abuse, because marriage in many ways is like a garden – if the participants will not fight day after day to keep it trim and beautiful, the wilderness will take over and smother its fairest flowers, and anyhow there is no proper appreciation of peace if it has not been preceded by a war.

This, of course, is not by way of condoning perpetual rows but when people are being besieged by a holocaust of prevailing misfortunes the row is vital to the make-up of married couples. The very wealthy rarely make scenes but then they do not take their obligations very seriously. Where men have to worry about next week's bills and women are tired after their long day's labours the germs of disquiet breed copiously and tiredness is responsible for more scenes than all the other natural failings put together. Men and women are not always prepared to make allowances and it is hard to blame them when money is scarce and the children's boots need new half-soles or when, unexpectedly, a civil bill arrives at the door to remind them of an extravagant but long-forgotten purchase.

It is always better to fight than to suffer in silence because silence at injustice leads to acceptance and marriage is one institution which can never be taken for granted. Sometimes, of course, when she gives out it is wiser to keep a shut mouth because it takes two to start a fight and one word always borrows another. A hardened old warrior, father of twenty children and battle-scarred from forty years of tumultous marriage once told me that when the woman begins to berate it is safer to ignore her, since if she is without fuel to further her denunciations the flame of her temper will quickly expire and she will be left frustrated and uncertain. But this is unfair, because she needs to let off steam and it is wrong to baulk her with silence. Instead the procedure should be to contradict her up to a point and to submit a partial plea of guilty. The defence must be spirited but throwing oneself at the mercy of the court with dumb supplication could easily result in the ear-splitting use of a fryingpan or in changing a woman of humour and temper to a befuddled unfortunate who doesn't know what to make out of her marriage. A row is worth the trouble and violence it begets if for nothing else than the making-up which comes afterwards when the couple fondly embrace and apologise for their evil tempers, when they endeavour to place all the blame upon one and completely acquit the other half, when they kiss and cuddle and promise each other that they will never have a row again – until the next time.

EIGHTEEN

THE LARGE WHITE DUCK

'Old soldiers like the leg of a duck'
(SONG)

SINCE the conception of the white turkey much fuss has been created concerning the qualities of this pampered bird. Much undeserved publicity has resulted from its outlandish activities while others of no less consequence have suffered from this unfair projectivity. In the barnyard he swaggers and struts like an emperor, forgetting that he is mere fowl the same as his contemporaries. The large white table duck waddles but this does not detract from his stature for when necks are stretched and feathers plucked it is performance at dinnertime that counts.

I have a profound respect for painters, for those who flick magic from palette to canvas and who capture forever an aspect or feature of a face. Yet when the covers of bastable ovens are lifted and the doors of cookers thrown open upon the golden rotundity of the large white table duck, one can hardly expect them to harness the thousand elements of pungency or vivify with mere paints and brushes the superb disinterestedness of tongue-tickling plumpness which glistens and crackles magnificent and alone.

There is something I always forget to do when glasses are full and friends are thrown together in conviviality in public houses and that is to uplift my beaker and propose a toast to rosy-faced old men who wore gaiters, at whose insistence flocks of specially-fed ducks were nurtured to table-ripeness and who had such a preference for ducks that they frequently called the more endearing specimens by their Christian names.

We often hear the expression: 'as hoarse as a duck' and

lest this be interpreted as a reflection, it should be remembered that neither Micawber nor Sam Weller were endowed with gifted voices and what might seem like hoarseness to us could well be the musical mating call of a handsome drake, beloved of many and as fiercely proud of his rendition as the grossest of barrel-chested operatic singers.

The large white table duck is no ordinary duck. Socially he is several flights above the common duck but you would never know it from his behaviour in the farmyard as compared with the hauteur of individuals like Rhode Island Red cocks and obstreperous ganders. His behaviour, to say the least, is gentlemanly. His temper, while perverse and uncertain at intrusion, is nevertheless even and fairly well-balanced most of the time. If there would seem to be bouts of occasional hysteria in the presence of marauding dogs he is merely bluffing his way out with as much bustle and commotion as possible. He is a friendly fellow and responds well to favour and I have known several instances where particular ducks have been adopted by small boys who succeeded in turning them into likeable pets and there are cited cases where they have been known to be as possessive and protective of their charges as dogs or even Nannies.

The large white duck does not know the meaning of the word cowardice. He will charge a foe ten times his size when he has to. He will not vacate a chosen seat upon the roadway no matter how suicidal his actions may seem. He will not be rushed and if his quacks are annoying at times who knows what strange duck-land lyricism is emanating from his brangling bill?

The large white duck, unlike his mongrel brethren, carries enough weight to do battle with well-peopled tables. The common duck has his work cut out for him to cope with a pair of appetites but the large white is deceptively wealthy in the matter of meat and has material enough to satisfy several. His crisp hide, soothed by a spoon of apple-sauce, is chewing matter as provocative as tobacco, and his breastmeat is beyond compare. Duck liver needs no introduction to those with sensitive tastes and the soup from duck's giblets is as nourishing as new milk. Boiled duck is somewhat uncommon but it is true to say that the white duck boils better than most fowl.

The old soldier is a man of few preferences and the world has taught him a considerable amount, for in his profession experience is dearly come by. But it will be noted, as we are told in the song, that he liked the leg of a duck, and many of those old songs which have survived more than a few wars are ingrained with truth. He may have liked Bologna pudding or sardines but the song does not say so. We only know that he liked the leg of a duck. It was Shakespeare who said that: '*foul deeds will rise, 'though all the earth o'erwhelm them to men's eyes.*' If this is so, they are slow enough in rising and the proof lies in the answers to these questions. How many of you have eaten a duck this year, a duck, mark you, not to mention the white duck? What is the frequency of white ducks on menu-cards? How many by persistent implication have fostered duck dinners? The truth is that none of you have and ducks together with drakes are now almost always reserved for the late dinners of tourists.

I can't speak for my readers but for myself I can most certainly say that on at least three occasions between now and Christmas my Sunday table will be enriched by the presence of the large white duck.

NINETEEN

MACKEREL

THERE is something deceitful and sneaky about herrings, hard to put the finger on but there is a consciousness of duplicity before and after they are eaten.

Salmon are pompous fellows who do not encourage prolonged relationships. Like Duffy's Circus, let me have them for one night, and one night only.

Eels should be left to ducks, and plaice reminds me of the man whose references are excellent but whose performance in practice is inadequate.

Whiting merely whittles the demanding appetite but mackerel is the merriest fellow of all for it is he who carried us through troublesome times and it is he who sated the hunger of true labour when wages were small and sports-coats the prerogative of the gentry.

Years before the advent of chipshops and snack-bars, they sailed in silver armadas through the blue eas of Munsters, celestial in design and remarkable for their humility, proud indeed to show that when God made mackerel he made them for poor people and if they did nothing more they kept many a small boy with curls on his head away from death's door in the horrendous years of famine.

Plump and swift and beautiful, he has always appeared when needed. No human artist from time's dawn outward could mould his impeccable symmetry, no poem pay tribute to his grace and shape, nor all the ballads of the Western seaboard do justice to his incomparable fertility.

An old woman with the wrinkled visage of a Potomac Indian comes to mind. She wears a brown shawl and over her face is the hard lean hunger of strife-filled years. She stands near the entrance to a market-place. In front of her are two boxes of mackerel and a heap of old newspapers.

Five for a shilling, fresh as a lover's kiss, and clean as the green ice of winter seas. She's out of sight now but never out of mind because, old as she was and poor as she was, she was the corner-stone of country commerce and, let it be to our eternal regret and shame, there are many of us who would be ashamed to be seen doing business with her now, but, God grant her a silver bed in Heaven, she gave the full of two frying pans for a shilling and she was the ultimate succour of the large family.

Times are always changing for the best, but haircuts to-day can cost a man as much as five shillings and what harm but there was a time when you could get an acre of hay cut for it.

Mackerel are not so much in demand any more. They still run in similar plenitude when breezes ruffle the frightening flats of the Atlantic but the craze now is for fillets of the more expensive provender although none of these featherweight tit-bits could hold its own for long with the mackerel.

I have eaten as many fish as the next man and I have my likes and dislikes. I will eat what is put in front of me and the only word of disapproval you'll hear from me is if my stomach informs me that we are being duped. I can take the rough with the smooth and I can employ my knife, my fork and my spoon to normal advantage.

I have dined in downstairs clubs in some queer quarters of the world where candlegrease formed outlandish patterns at the bases of artistic holders and where the talk centred about artistic issues which were supposed to be of importance. I have understood a good deal and bluffed my way through with commendable invention when I was out of my depth but for me, truly, the great moment in life happened at the bottom of a long table with a mackerel on my plate. Conversation belonged to another world, but there was orchestral accompaniment when steel wrangled with delph. Afterwards when the table was cleared and the crockery put away, a man could pat his belly and whisper to himself: 'Thanks be to God for mackerel!'

TWENTY

CANISTER-KICKING

WHEN the moon rides high and stars glitter like Irish threepenny-bits, the most insignificant of sounds can have a jarring effect on the quiet tenor of the night. Carolling cats cavort on shed-tops and the haunting sound of their love-songs frequently falls on ears which twitch unappreciatively with murderous intent. Coarser melodies fortified by the rugged harmony of drunken chorusers shatter the nerve centres of exhausted providers but soothing is the lonely clip-clop of a wandering pony who has strayed far from the barren fields of his prison or stolen from the cruelty of an ungrateful master.

The night has mysterious powers but the weirdest by far is its strange knack of investing commonplace noises with personality and character which are totally absent in the bright bustle of daytime. I am not referring to the scurrilous outrages of vandals who abuse the protection that night affords them. Let us instead pay tribute to more delicate things.

For me, the clatter of a kicked canister is a poem and while its first effect must create intolerance and prejudice, we must show a little fortitude and a little patience, for he who ponders a little is rewarded with a rich harvest of luxurious emotions and to relax is to have poetry poured over you from the bottomless kettle of remembrance.

Canisters are kicked in different ways by different people. There is the rebellious rattle caused by the shoe of the baker's apprentice whose eyes are still half-closed. For him, a canister on the way to work is as important as the proverbial black cat to the superstitious bookmaker. Alone he treads the dismal street, a young contender in the old game of the world, a small man in the mighty void of night. An empty canister glimmers under a bright moon. He is about to pass it by, but then the great urge which distinguishes man from the animal surges within him. He draws back his leg and kicks. Contact is made and the canister is sent spinning across the roadway. Suddenly the world is a brighter place and instead of rueful mutterings about his unhappy lot, the shrill whistle of a marching song disturbs the still folds of night and he tramps to his labours filled with the importance of his calling, an idealist, a builder without whose contribution the bellies of the world would rumble with hunger and the teeth of thousands topple from the ills of haphazardly-mixed dough.

More joyful still is the kick of the young man in love because he aspires to art. Not for him the casual swipe, but the full-blooded kick of the suitor whose attentions are being seriously considered by the girl of his dreams. He walks away from her door after leaving her home for the first time. For the first time in his life, too, he is conscious of the antics of a crazy moon seeking sanctuary amid fragments of torn cloud. His heart is full and he longs to express himself in a fashion befitting his proud situation. His eye alights upon the canister and with a gleeful whoop he draws a mighty kick. The canister soars high into the air but before it reaches the ground, like Setanta he is waiting and again he lofts it skywards. Having written his poem, he goes home to sleep, to dream, to plan.

Elderly men with ponderous paunches and heads of grey thatch are not above canister-kicking. Their activities, naturally enough, in this respect are confined to backalleys and deserted laneways where prying eyes are not likely to register their odd movements and loquacious tongues left without fodder to spread word of their remarkable activities.

Empty cigarette-boxes are eminently kickable at all times, but they are hardly likely to sponsor release from ponderous problems or cloying responsibilities, and while one is frequently tempted to draw at the occasional banana-skin it is doubtful if the same satisfaction will be forth-coming from such unresponsive discards.

I do not advocate canister-kicking lightly but I do not recommend it as a form of occupational therapy either. You kick canisters or you don't. If you kick canisters you know that it can be a rewarding pastime. You never forget that you, too, were once a juvenile delinquent, that canis-ter-kicking is as necessary as leap-frog, wrestling, yodelling, shouting, whistling and all other types of high jinks.

There are no high-kick or long-kick championships for canister-kickers but a man knows from the amount of pleasure derived from the kick how far he has travelled in this unique method of expression.

It is a proud and secret art because few can be trusted and none but old friends who have travelled jointly over the years on private excursions for porter dare to indulge in each other's presence. Canister-kicking in private is the last athletic prerogative of district court Justices, gardai, doc-tors, schoolmasters, curates, busdrivers and others who must always preserve a façade of dignity when under the public eye, but from any angle you like the man who passes a kickable canister without indulging is not much of a man.

TWENTY ONE

A BIT OF A LONGING

I T is commonly believed that very old people, on the verge of departure from these climes, are overcome by sudden longings for unusual types of food. This may be prompted by inside information from reliable sources on the other side, because different journeys require different dishes, and it is no disadvantage to have a slant in the direction one is likely to be taking.

The gratification of such whims is the least that loved ones might fulfil, because, after all, they will not be called upon again by the outgoing parties and, regardless of the difficulties presented, no effort should be spared to furnish these final solaces.

I once heard of an old woman who expressed a longing for a piece of a kid's liver shortly after she was anointed for the third time. A hurried consultation took place among those at the bedside and interested parties were appointed to institute a search. There were no goats in the locality, and it was decided to slaughter a lamb. The liver was fried quickly and, while the old lady was not completely satisfied, it proved nevertheless to be of considerable assistance to her because she lived to die another day and surprised all and sundry by burying several neighbours who had bought black stockings for her funeral.

We are not expected to believe, of course, that a man who asks for the wing of a chicken is on his way to join the angels nor, indeed, is the man who breathes his ultimate wish for ice-cream on his way to a place where no overcoats will be needed, but there is reason to expect that the man who asks for devilled eggs has no illusions about his eventual destination.

When an old man sits up in the bed before the last gasp

and demands that he be provided with a plate of giblet soup at a moment's notice, the dependents are automatically absolved of all responsibility, because the unfortunate individual has left it go too late and it must be conceded in all fairness to those involved that he has nobody but himself to blame. In ordinary circumstances when the writing is on the wall well beforehand, it pays to make preparation for every contingency. Sometimes the demand may be for as little as a few slices of brown bread or a tin of kippered herrings but there is always the outside chance that a stuffed sheep's heart or a saucerful of cockles will be insisted upon. Neither should surprise be shown if an old man rolls his eyes around in his head and announces with great fervour that he would truly love to stick his head into a bucketful of semolina.

Last minute requests, however, are only part of the great range of desire, for every age has its own share of longing. A man was once asked by a District Court judge what explanation he could offer for being drunk and disorderly on the occasion of his being arrested. His answer was less elaborate but more effective than any counsel could offer. 'It all began, boss,' he said, 'when I got the longin' for a few pints.'

Expectant mothers are to be forgiven all longings. A young woman of my acquaintance woke up one morning at four o'clock and told her husband that she had a terrible longing for a plate of corned beef and cabbage. The husband, courageously enough, shook himself out of slumber, rose, dressed and mounted his bicycle. He then cycled four miles to town where he routed a butcher, of unstable emotions, from profound sleep. He succeeded in procuring a delicate pound of silverside. It is only fair to add that the butcher was sympathetic when the full facts were made known to him. Not only did he escort the young man out of town but rendered him invaluable assistance in stealing a head of well-matured cabbage from the garden of the local Garda sergeant. Arriving at his home the husband located a saucepan and watched its every agitation as soon as it reached boiling point. Proudly he bore the finished product to the bedroom, only to be told curtly that she had changed her mind and wanted a stewed rack-chop instead.

A deep longing is a tragic thing and saddest of all are the boys and girls who make up in far countries to see a red dawn breaking over a strange horizon. There is the hasty dressing for work and the gulped breakfast. Under the cheerful 'Good morning!' given to an impersonal bus-conductor there is the wistful remembering and the heart-breaking longing for the immortal faces of home.

TWENTY TWO

BACON AND CABBAGE

LEST the wrong impression be given, let me say at once that the type of bacon I have in mind is homecured. It has been hanging from the ceiling for months, and when you cut a chunk from it there is the faintest of golden tinges about its attractive shapeliness.

When this type of bacon is boiling with its old colleague, white cabbage, there is a gurgle from the pot that would tear the heart out of a hungry man, and when the woman of the house lifts the cover to see that all is well underneath, there is an odour of such winning appeal and long-range sensitivity that men working in fields hundreds of yards away could tell you how far the cooking has progressed, or if the cabbage is still a bit stringy and needs another quarter of an hour before the whistle sounds and tools are downed for the major meal of the day.

Hams, gams and spare-ribs are spoken of whenever the dinner is a bit long in coming up, but for all their appeal and for all their well-deserved popularity, they belong under the head of accessory. They are only the means by which the stomach arrives at complete appreciation of bacon and cabbage. They are competent and they are honest, obliging foods without pretension and, while disparagement is not even remotely intended, it must truthfully be said that they exist chiefly for the gratification of transient obsessions and under no circumstances are they embodied to grapple with the consistent appetite. They are in the same class as occupational junior footballers, great upon the occasion but not empowered to cope with the professional stomach over a pre-determined period.

Good bacon is judged by the amount of juice which escapes down the side of the mouth during mastication.

There is no cooking involved – at least not in the strict sense. Steaks, chops and omelettes need constant attention and even then the desired effect is not always achieved. With bacon the only problem is keeping the cover on the pot, because, when it gets together with cabbage there is any amount of intimate gurgling, murmuring and explosive chuckling, with the result that they are liable to raise the roof if the cover is too small for the pot. Apart from the volume of cabbage-water lost on occasions like this, there is the extra danger of smoke – a natural enemy to decent flavours of all kinds.

Time was when any man passing the way was welcome to a seat at all tables. If he was a stranger, his shyness was taken into consideration and no invitation was extended. A place was found to be vacant, and he was lifted, together with his chair, to within operational distance of the fare. If business was brisk and no room was available at table, a full plate was placed on his lap and with the aid of knife and fork he found little difficulty in disposing of the offering.

To present a truly representative picture of the joys belonging to bacon and cabbage, it is necessary to depict a country kitchen at midday when men with strong boots and corduroy trousers place caps upon knees and sit down with sighs of gratitude to dinner. Heaped plates appear quickly. A pot of spuds is poured on to a special sack or cloth in the table centre. The idea here is to prove that bread-plates are totally unnecessary and that they contrive only to produce extra labour for the woman of the house. So great is the quantity and so high the mound created by the potatoes that men sitting at opposite sides of the table fail to create normal conversation until the meal is well-advanced and the heap of spuds reduced to eye-level.

I remember, years ago, to have been cycling to a sports-meeting at CarraigKerry on the borders of Limerick. A shower of rain persisted in knocking at my bare head and new clothes, so I jumped off the bicycle to take shelter under a cluster of trimmed white-thorn which foreheaded the low whitewashed wall in front of a cottage. Needless to mention there was a mother in the cottage. I was hauled in out of harm's way and put sitting near the fire. The family was at its dinner.

A voice asked: 'Will you chance a forkful o'bacon and a mouthful o'cabbage?'

'No, thanks!' I said. 'I had my dinner an hour ago.'

I was put sitting between the woman of the house and her father-in-law, an old man with a friendly wink in both eyes. After the first small mouthful I did more than hold my own with my competitors, which goes to prove the contention that growing boys are always hungry, expecially after they've had their dinners.

Nobody is questioning the fact that the world would still succeed in orbiting if bacon and cabbage was no longer eaten, but few will deny that the world to-day contains more threats to the sanctity of the family than ever before. Gone are the days when every ceiling was festooned with flitches, when men relied upon their own initiative and there was little whimpering about the responsibilities of the State, when stomach bottles were novelties rather than necessities, when old men and old women were loved and not neglected, when men appreciated simple fare and thanked the providence of God for the health and strength that gave them appetite.

TWENTY THREE

CORNS

I ONCE knew a woman who wore out three bicycles in search of a cure for corns.

She spent the price of a Bubble-car on guaranteed remedies, when all that she really required was a larger size in shoes.

I heard of a man who won seventy cups for waltzing but he would have forfeited them all unconditionally if his corns gave him a moment's peace.

Whenever I see a really beautiful, well-coiffured, immaculately-dressed woman, I always arrive at one of two conclusions. She is extraordinarily wealthy or, on the other hand, she has very little to do at home. Similarly when I see a stout woman sitting on an upturned box at a point-to-point meeting I hazard the guess that her shoes are too tight for her, or that she forgot to look after her corns that morning before leaving home.

Corns thrive nowhere with such exultant disregard for man's comforts as under the patronage of poorly-fitting shoes and additionally a man is never conscious of his corns when he patters about on bare feet. Corns have often dictated the humour of a man's day and not infrequently instituted the beginnings of minor law suits because many regard the act of standing upon a corn accidentally under the same light as assault and battery, badgering and obstruction and it would not surprise me to learn that the error made by Napoleon in attempting to subdue Russia was brought about as a result of wearing tight-fitting boots.

Until recently I have had little sympathy for those who suffer from corns. Frequently after football matches, where men are compelled to stand for hours in congestion, I have scoffed at older colleagues who sat themselves relievedly upon convenient window-sills after leaving the football pitch and proceeded, without regard for caution, to unlace their shoes. The sighs and other ejaculations of pleasure heard upon the occasion were proof of the relief enjoyed and we laughed, some of us, in derision at these comical situations, unconscious of unforeseen martyrdom and blissfully unaware of the latter-day development of constricted paunches which come with ripening of age.

The era of the casual corn-cutter belongs to history because these days there are as many cures as there are corns and the neighbour whose forte was corncutting is no longer called in.

There are many who may say boastfully that they have never been afflicted by corns, but in the toes of each of us is the nucleus of a horrifying harvest and all that is required is a pair of new shoes to bring them forth. Man for the most part is safe enough from the scourge because if he is once bitten by an ill-advisedly purchased shoe he will lower his sights for future occasions, but woman will never see the light. She will persist, God love her!, in carrying the day, and admittedly it is hard to burden a shapely white foot with a shoe that looks cumbersome. It is unfair to expect a woman, whose figure is preserved in spite of maturity, to wear flat sensible shoes. If she picks up a corn or two in the process it is a churlish husband who would not bend his knee to bring her relief. It was a wise man who said that nothing should ever be thrown away. The derelict razor-blade, unwanted and unsung, can play a powerful part in extremity and whatever is said about peculiar and particular cures, corn-paring is as classic an example of practical art as any.

The principle which would have us credit the fallacy that any instrument which pares a pencil will pare a corn has seen to its own share of sore toes. Wood is dispassionate and unmoving but a sensitive toe is liable to unite with its four brethren into a strong assault force which could readily loosen a tooth in the mouth of the administrator.

Never before, in the history of mankind, have such advances been made in all the sciences but man in his blindness has overlooked evils under his nose. The corn will always be with us so let there be a school devoted to corns. Let there be an investigation made as to their culture and origin. Let the habits of the dormant corn be brought to light and let our womenfolk fulfil their feminine, and fanciful, indulgences without suffering and discomfort. Let stout men stand with impunity and let us, for once and all, clear the air in respect of corns.

TWENTY FOUR

GEESE

RECENTLY, while dining with an elderly friend, he kicked my shin under the table when the first course of goose's soup was put in front of us. Apprehensively we exchanged looks and tasted the concoction.

'All this is very fine,' my friend said to the waiter, 'but where's the goose?'

Waiter: 'What goose?'

Friend: 'The goose that was used to make the soup.'

Waiter: 'The soup came in a package, sir.'

Friend: 'It is a matter of complete indifference to me how the soup came. What concerns me is that somewhere along the line there was a goose involved in all this. What has happened to him?'

Waiter: 'I'm sure there is breast of goose in the deepfreeze, sir.'

Friend: (SNEERINGLY): 'Roasted, no doubt, in a bastable oven?'

Waiter: (HAUGHTILY): I'm sure I don't know what you mean, sir.'

We resumed our meal in silence, but it made me think. In order to make you think, too, I will try to put you in the picture, and in order to do that it will be necessary for me to brief you with regard to the characteristics of the goose in question.

In case I am accused of prejudice latterly, let me say at the outset that the goose is an ordinary one and in no way exceptional or different from the average of his fellows.

As I see him, he is plucked, stuffed and sewn and sitting luxuriantly in a large pan. A woman with a spoon is ladling scalding brown gravy over the golden breast, which is plump and in danger of bursting at its seams. There are enchanting lumps of steaming pandy bursting through the waistcoat pockets of this goose, and let me say here and now, that there was never a man, from toddler to dotard, who could resist the urge to rifle said pockets and cram his mouth with the plunder. It is a picture I always bring to mind when I hear people talking about cocktail sausages.

There are no statistics available, but you may be sure that the consumption of geese has dropped irrevocably. If you don't believe me, wait until you are coming out from Mass next Sunday. Stop the first stranger you meet and ask him truthfully how long it has been since he had a goose for his dinner. If he gives you a look that links you with lunacy, tell him you are making a Gallup poll. You know, as well as I do, that he'll shake his head sadly and tell you that he hasn't made a mouth-organ out of a goose's thigh since his mother went to Dublin to live with her son-in-law.

We almost wiped out the rabbit with myxomatosis, but we are killing the goose with indifference. I will most certainly grant you that no man in his right mind will turn his back on a plate of goose's breast, golden sauce and breath-taking stuffing, but how many of us, these days, are qualified to judge the points of a goose? One can easily be duped by an old warrior who has grandchildren in every parish in Munster and whose carcase couldn't be roasted by the fires of hell. There was, and still is, a sacred sect of old women, in out-of-the-way places, who rear geese like they would children, to whom it is a matter of personal pride that their produce be relished and their name for fair dealing upheld.

It is a sad day for the world when goose's soup is relegated to the package. The next thing we'll hear of is powdered chops. It is no wonder, indeed, that crime is on the increase and teenagers are feigning disgust over periwinkles. It is strange, in a world where men shave every day, that a roast goose is as rare as a whalebone corset, and imported pretenders, such as turkey-cocks, are the gentry of the moment.

Goose's blood is another delicacy which our aspiring chefs would do well to learn about. I don't see any reason why I should divulge the formula here, but a courteous letter to the Editor will reveal the secret. Caution is no harm when we remember the ingenious methods used in the stealing of the atom, and if they didn't stop at murder over that, what would they not do over goose's blood?

Many of our greatest recipes went down with our emigrant ships; recipes that did not consist of luxurious contents but rather the garnishing of simple things to console palates that had endured indignity heaped upon indignity.

We were eating geese in Ireland when Drake was chewing eels at Plymouth, but change is everywhere. Grandfathers with majestic paunches who used to carry great cargoes of porter with the dignity of sailing ships, and who used to give half-crowns to small boys, are gone from the scene. They would never have tolerated the absence of roast geese from the table. Perhaps it is just as well that they are not here to witness the last twitchings of a generation where men's stomachs are growing smaller and their voices louder; a generation doomed to an end bristling with flatulence and gastritis; a generation that has failed because it has placed the tin can before the goose.

TWENTY FIVE

ENEMIES OF THE REPUBLIC

A NATION, like a bagpipes, depends on its belly, and if our food supplies are corrupted or contaminated, it is time to take stock of ourselves. It is time to seriously assess our strength and marshal our forces, time to wage wholesale war on insidious factors which would undermine the health of our manhood. Let us leave no stone unturned in the purge, and let us begin with that sacriligeous smart Alec – the stuffed tomato.

Try to picture him sitting pompously on a plate, with his buttons undone, and his vermilion but vulgar colouring outshining that of his more sober contemporaries. The rasher, the egg and the sausage are not showoffs, but then, in their particular cases, there is no need for pretension. The kidney is hardly noticeable but he makes himself felt in the closing stages when quality counts. The stuffed tomato takes pride of place because he thinks he is the be-all and end-all of the meal, but, fortunately, the stomach is not so easily fooled. He is the least popular in the cast of a mixed grill, but, by fraud and deception, he received major billing. The cure for his inexcusable snobbery is to eat him promptly without savouring his taste or his temper. Wash him down quickly with common water and turn attention fully to the respectable occupants of the plate.

Prejudice is more malicious than the collective enemies of truth, and, lest I be accused of harbouring same, permit me to say that I bear no prejudice whatsoever against cucumber sandwiches. All I want to do is to expose, for once and for all, the myth that would have us believe them to be sandwiches of substance. Tasteless and without proper body, they have managed to escape detection for years. I have seen grown men show preference for cucumber before ham, chicken and roast beef sandwiches, for no other reason than trying to show what smart fellows they were.

Potted pea soup is another vagabond of the table with nothing to recommend it except its colour. It is not the kind of soup you would dip your bread in to, and it most certainly is not the kind of soup you would give a man who has spent a heartbreaking day thinning mangolds or scouring dykes. By all means, let the cat have it, or, if the fancy takes you, boil a duck in it, but do not put it in front of a man who has spent the previous night at an engagement party.

Fried eggs I will always tolerate, because these are fellows of extraordinary calibre who have passed the most rigis tests and settled harmoniously in the most uncivil of stomachs. However, fried bananas are a different satchel of goods altogether, and it is against these that I make protest. If I was given fried bananas, I would not merely go on hunger-strike: I would assault the responsible party and to hell with the consequences, because I can think of no greater personal indignity. Fried bananas, indeed! Give me fried gizzards, or give me fried bread, but do not reduce me to the level of idiocy altogether.

There is another equally menacing mixture, which I have studied closely for years, and that is the terrible concoction which is labelled shrimp cocktail. No selfrespecting fish should be associated with withcraft of this sort, and one can be assured that, if the shrimp had any say in the matter, he would settle for a respectable burial in the gut of a cock-salmon. The only logical conclusion one can come to is that the cocktail was invented to take the taste out of the shrimps.

We got peanut paste from America, but our grand-mothers destroyed it with farmer's butter. We have kept chop-suey and Maryland chicken at bay this long while, and the red wines of France will have their work cut out for them if they are to usurp the black porter of our fathers.

But, from all corners, we are threatened. A foothold is all the enemy needs for a stranglehold. I wonder if giblet soup will be over-awed by tomato soup, or what way will the whole sorry situation sort itself in the end? It does not bear thinking about.

If there would appear to be a note of alarm in the few observations I have made in dealing with these poltroons of the dining-hall, my intent has been realised, because the youth of the country must be considered, and unless new generations are forewarned a day will come when small boys with short trousers will insist on napkins when they sit at table. Worse still, the young men of the land will turn up their noses at proud fish like mackerel. Aristocrats like pig's-heads will be frowned upon, and noodle soup will threaten Irish Stew.

Who, of our present generation, has gnawed a young drake's windpipe, or argued over the merits of salt mackerel? Who has savoured the chill delight of cooling butter-milk in the dry days of summer, or who has roasted fresh mushrooms on wine-red coals? Not many, because innovations have murdered our imaginations, and few house-wives of to-day could survive without the assistance of the package and the tin-can.

So, on with your bonnets, young women of the Republic! Unite, and repel the impostors, and next week, for our dinners, give us something we can get our teeth into, so that the healthy odours of yesterday will come back to us the moment we open the door.

TWENTY SIX

SAUSAGE-ROLLS

THE WORLD, we are told, should be a happy place. Harmony should prevail and tolerance should be the gospel of to-day. Criticism should never enter, and allowances should be made, at all times, for the shortcomings of others.

I, for one, heartily concur with sentiments of this nature, and therefore it is with reluctance that I am compelled to make a few justifiable observations, so please let it be remembered afterwards that they started it themselves when they invented sausage-rolls.

Many frauds have been perpetrated under the guise of improvisation, but none, to my mind, with such cheek and impertinence as the sausage-roll.

I am, unequivocally, on the side of the mother who preserves the remains of Sunday's joint, and presents it with the aid of accessories under a different title on Monday. Maybe it is my constitution, or maybe I am an allergist at heart but, whatever it is, I refuse to be associated with sausage-rolls. Not that I've never indulged. I have eaten as many sausage-rolls as the next fellow, but they are deceitful scoundrels at best, fooling the uninitiated stomach and giving the impression to this gullible tract that all will be well until the next meal. I have risen from the table, glutted to the gills, after sausage-rolls, only to be faced with acute hunger an hour later. Frequently I have been compelled to request a sandwich from an impressionable barmaid, thereby giving the wife a bad name and acquiring an undeserved reputation for gluttony at the same time. I might add, too, that heartburn and flatulence were black strangers to me before I was tempted by an innocuous-looking sausage-roll. Of course, I have nobody but myself to blame. A friend of mine, a man of considerable will-power and independent thought, was told recently by his wife that she intended to surprise him with sausage-rolls for his supper.

'You're wrong!' he stated calmly. 'I'm having potato-cakes for my tea.'

Perhaps it was the way he said it, or maybe his eyes were narrow slits, like those of Randolph Scott or Peter Lorre before they cut loose. Whatever it was, his forecast was correct. He had potato-cakes for his supper. The same gentleman told me afterwards, in confidence, that he wouldn't have a sausage-roll under his roof for all the minerals in Tynagh.

Lest people think I am soured and bitter, I will present damning evidence without further delay.

A junior football team, of which I am a proud supporter, was engaged in an evening game with an old traditional foe. We led by two points until the last minute when a hopping ball refused to hop and instead passed between the obliging legs of our goalkeeper. We all make mistakes. Perhaps few are as conscious of this fact as myself, but I felt constrained, nevertheless, to ask the goalkeeper why he made the cardinal error of not keeping his legs together. He told me he had a touch of gripe.

'You must have eaten the wrong kind of meat,' I said, casually, as I walked away.

'Sausage-rolls!' he cried after me.

The other goalkeeper, a respectable scholarly-looking boy with nice manners, was leaving the pitch shortly afterwards.

'Would you mind,' I said, 'if I asked you a few personal questions?'

'Not at all!' he replied, with infinite charm.

'What did you have for tea this evening?'

He cogitated, if I might use the word, for a moment or two.

'Why,' he said, 'I had bread and butter, a cup of tea, and two boiled duckeggs.'

He had, I might add, brought off several brilliant saves during the hour. If further evidence is needed, my own infrequent internal disorders after sausage-rolls are positive proof of what I say.

The time has come to draw the line, and one of these days I am going to do it. In all justice, however, it must be conceded that there is room in the world for sausage-rolls, too. There is nothing wrong with an odd sausage-roll at picnics, or hen-parties, but if we are to have sanity in the world, the dignity of man must be the first consideration. His will must be buttressed with healthy foods, not out-landish oddities that some precocious schoolgirl cooked up for devilment. If women exist who feel that their worlds would fall apart if sausage-roll making was prohibited, let them bake them by all means, but let them eat them them-selves, or give them to the hens, and, indeed, unless I am greatly mistaken, no Rhode Island Red or White Sussex worth her salt will put up with them either. In addition, sausages were designed for the frying-pan. They are fellows who have enough to put up with, what with having to associate with greasy chips night after night and playing second fiddle to the rasher and the egg on the morning table. They belong with mixed grills, who will tolerate any sort of company, and remember, too, that it is a lot easier to mix the makings of a few pancakes than it is to manufacture a menagerie of sausage-rolls.

TWENTY SEVEN

TURNIPS

'Don't feed him with soft turnips, take him down to
yon green lawn,
And 'tis then that you might be able for to plough
the Rocks of Bawn.'
(SONG)

THERE are several schools of thought concerning the preparation, cooking and serving of turnips.

An old agricultural labourer of my acquaintance would have it that turnips no matter what their disguise, are only fit for cows. He maintains that they are full of water, entirely without real substance and fraudulent even when they appear with such acceptable companions as beef, mutton and pork.

I disagree with him, although I respect his opinion, for stewed turnips are as appetising a dish as one could hope to meet up with in a season of dinners, and, furthermore, turnips are easily come by since you can possess an ass-rail of turnips for less than is required to purchase a secondhand golf club.

I do not support the claim that turnips should be eaten as frequently as cabbage, nor have they the iron determination of parsnips, but a turnip stewed on farflung occasions, or the odd boiled turnip with a bit of bacon is not to be laughed off, and indeed, personally speaking, I will take turnips without demur so long as the responsible parties know where to draw the line. Turnips have their place and must be kept there because truthfully a regular diet of turnips will not result in many second row forwards or tug-o'-war teams and I have yet to hear a centenarian attribute his longevity to turnips. But stewed turnips are different. It is as if the turnip had changed character completely in the process. Stewed turnips are as enjoyable and palatable as cauliflowers or carrots and have at least as many fans as beans. Yet I stress the danger involved, and my old agricultural friend is right in many respects.

There is the story he told me about a farmer's boy who was fed almost entirely on turnips for twenty consecutive years. After years of obedient and docile service, he one day expressed a desire for a piece of boiling beef. It was given to him, with soup and onions, not long after and he did justice to the fare. Hardly an hour had passed when he appeared in the farmer's kitchen, wearing his new suit, with the tidings that he was leaving immediately for England. When I asked my agricultural friend to account for such unpremeditated behaviour, he was fortright in his answer. 'No base,' he said. 'Twenty years of turnips is no base for meat. The meat went to his head and you can put it all down to turnips.' 'Aren't you rather inclined,' I argued, 'to victimize the turnip?' 'No!' he replied, 'turnips is turnips. Give them to cows but don't give me no boiled turnips. A man's bones needs oil and there is no oil in turnips, not as much as would grease the joints of a safety pin.'

The man's active dislike of turnips is not without reason for we have seen the effects of the sustained diet of same on his friend. I have consulted others on the same subject and I have yet to find a person prepared to make a stand on behalf of turnips. While there is adequate support, there is no adamantine support. One old woman said to me: 'The first feed of 'em is alright but after that they gets aggrawatin'!' It would seem, therefore, from these few observations that turnips belong in that unhappy category where there is neither for nor against. There never will be bitter argument over turnips, or no blows struck. Apart from '*The Rocks of Bawn*', which is purely defamatory, no song has appeared in their praise and no poem to immortalise them. Maybe so, but it could be said that their immortality is in their seed and their songs in the boiling pot but the turnip is not a loud-voiced nor a raucous singer and his speeches in his own defence are not recorded. The turnip is a hummer, and hummers, while soothing and innocous, are not singers and, unfair as it may seem, they must as a consequence be ignored, on these particular grounds.

I don't know why I should have written about turnips at all but I suppose it is partly from a feeling of endeavouring to prove parity in all things and also with the hope that there are people somewhere in the world who like turnips better than they like anything else. It is not too much to expect. There are people who prefer uncles to aunts and exceptional people who prefer pickled cow's tongue to roast pheasant. Looking back I feel that turnips may have been abused because they should never be allowed to attain to ripe old age and massive rotundity. If small boys were as active as they should be, turnips would never be permitted to age or soften. They would be unearthed in the sweetness of adolescence by grimy hands and eaten like apples. But that day is gone, too, and too many shillings find their way into the pockets of our unadventurous youngsters. There are young lads these days to whom a green field is a desert, a wood a foreign country and a river a place which has neither a beginning nor an ending, so the next time a pampered adolescent asks you for the price of a pear, send him out into the country, far out, where his appetite will leave him no choice but to forage for turnips.

TWENTY EIGHT

BACK-STUDS

ONE of the most interesting men I have ever known was a traveller for back-studs, front-studs, mousetraps, hooks-and-eyes, assorted zip-fasteners and sundries.

He had a bulbous red nose, which was deeply indebted for its size and colour to ten-year-old Irish whiskey. One of his calls was to a small shop where I was a constant visitor. He would reel off his list of wares and wait solemnly for his order. If no business was forthcoming, he would stare at the shopkeeper incredulously. 'Son,' he would say, 'you may not want hooks-and-eyes or spools of 36 white cotton. You can drag along without corn plasters and tuppeny jotters. But no man can afford to be without back-studs!'

At the time I was conscious only of the man's intriguing proboscis, but the years proved that he was an experienced man of the world because nobody who is attached to the unattached collar can do without a back-stud.

I have lost school badges, pencil-toppers, erasers, tooth-picks and Pioneer pins and they have always appeared again in unexpected places, but I have yet to recover a lost back-stud.

Loss of any kind, in itself, is relatively tragic, but he who loses a back-stud is himself lost. Supermarkets and Fancy Emporiums are cluttered with fortunes in stock, but just try one of them for a back-stud and watch the expression of amazement on the face of the assistant. A barrel of gun-powder would seem like a more reasonable request. You won't come across back-studs in the gilded premises of main thoroughfares. You have to leave the beaten track and search for the small shop. It doesn't have to be a Fancy Goods shop and don't be put off by the sight of brussels sprouts in a basket outside the door. You won't have to repeat your request, because the small man with the brown five-quarter length shopcoat will, in a trice, place two or three cards of different species in front of you. You will choose one at random, anxious to be away, for upholders of unattached collars are not hagglers, and for the most part they are men who hurry, hence the high incidence of loss in regard to back-studs. But hurry, while it hastens the dodgy craft of commerce does not search for the source of the contrary wind or retrace the fruitless forests of misadventure looking for the pathway which is neither devious nor divisible. Brief as is my tenure in this vexatious sphere, I have learned one truth and that is more than most learn in a lifetime. The truth is this – if you are purchasing a back-stud and if the merchant offers you five for a shilling, don't fall into the trap of refusing his offer. Take them and you'll have made extensive inroads into the expansive land of truth. A man cannot have enough back-studs. Once after a hilarious wedding breakfast I bought three dozen from a stall-holder who knows a sucker when she sees one. She may have thought that she was having the better of me but, for a pittance, I was thirty-six back-studs the wealthier.

'Now,' I said to myself, 'I will never be short of a back-stud again!'

How wrong my prophecy proved to be. Within a year or to be exact ten minutes before I was due to depart to a dress dance I mislaid the last of the fortuitous thirty-six. I searched. My wife searched. Friends and neighbours searched, but to no avail. I was indeed fortunate that the womenfolk of the party succeeded in prevailing upon a reluctant but impressionable young Civic Guard who happened to be passing and who at the time was unattached and could hardly refuse the tearful requests of so many anguished women. It was a lesson to him, and to me, too, but regardless of the depth of my stockpile I have been caught napping repeatedly on occasions such as five minutes before last Mass and upon the morning of important appointments.

Back-studs have contributed to a large percentage of domestic discord. Rash accusations are made, and blame is often laid where it least belongs – but men will never learn. The guilty party, his own improvidence, is never made to pay the price and it is the small boy who receives the unexpected slap on the behind for sins which he has yet to commit. Account for the disappearance of the back-stud and you have accounted for certain of man's unaccountable prejudices. I remember once, while a guest in a house a long way from home, to be pained at the erratic and bestial behaviour of the lord and master of the establishment towards his delph and cutlery. He slammed and banged without provocation and I felt that it might be my fault for having routed him out of bed so early to enable me comply with the native transport schedule. Later, when he bent to enter his car, preparatory to driving me to the station, I noticed that his collar was about as stable as a cork in rough water and I realised that the unfortunate man was more to be pitied than blamed.

The back-stud has a lot to answer for, but then the back-stud has never been taken as seriously as it should be. Women will sweat till the witching hours of Saturday night but women will also persist in misplacing the occasional back-stud.

TWENTY NINE

PIGS' HEADS

Earth has not anything to show more fair:
Dull would he be of soul who could pass by
A sight so touching in its majesty.

WORDSWORTH

LIFE is funny and life is short, but life would be a lot funnier if it were any longer, and life, I very much fear, and the good things in it, are not availed of fully, and the tragedy is that people pass on to the next life without tasting the true pleasures of this one and all because of excessive interest in monetary and other inconsequential affairs.

To illustrate my point, let me tell the story of the jackdaw and the sparrow. It was Christmas and the river was frozen over. The jackdaw tried vainly to break the ice with his beak. He was thirsty but the ice was thick, and, knock as he would, the ice remained firm. A sparrow arrived on the scene and studied the jackdaw cautiously for a while.

'Any hope of a drink?' he asked, when he saw that the jackdaw meant him no harm.

'Nothing doing!' said the jackdaw. 'I've been knocking here for a half an hour, and no answer so far.'

'Hard lines!' the sparrow agreed. 'I'm piping with the thirst myself.'

'I could do with a drink too,' said the jackdaw.

'Ah my friend,' said the sparrow, 'we didn't drink it while we had it!'

The moral of this story is that men die without even once having tasted pig's head. They might have done so if they had bothered to pace themselves in the race of life but cupidity and lack of insight disabled their faculties and deprived them of proper judgment when it came down to important things.

I have little admiration for men who make millions, but I have respect for a man who shows restraint when he is faced with a plate of pig's head and cabbage and I don't care what others may think, but for me a pig's head exhibited in a window has as winning a way with it as a platter of engagement rings or a regiment of chops.

Hot or cold, the pig's head is a man's food. Put him with any company you like – kale, cabbage or turnips – and he will hold his own because, like all true nobility, he can mix with king or commoner. To those who view him for the first time, his appearance may be against him but to close one's eyes and savour the first unforgettable mouthful is an experience which nobody should forego and, indeed, if housewives had any sense of justice, no child would be permitted to reach the use of reason without having first tasted pig's cheek.

If I were a prospective employer and if I were interviewing a man for a position of trust, I would not fall into the trap of asking him the usual unrevealing questions such as where he went to school and the extent of his past experience in relation to the job. There is no more reliable guide in the assessment of a man's character than to ask him bluntly what his opinions are with regard to pig's head. If he frowns and shakes his head, the interview should be terminated there and then, but if he smiles and tells you there is nothing in the world like it, you have a man who will not only meet the requirements of the job but who will without question enhance the position by filling it, a man who loves his mother and is not ashamed of his poor relations – in short, a man of breeding and discernment.

The pig's head is equally suited to large families and small. For the large families a whole pig's head provides a satisfying, digestable meal so that when the time comes for vacating the table there are no cries of complaint.

For the small family, the remains of the meal may be put aside until nightfall. A safe place of concealment should be the primary concern because neighbours, regardless of their honesty, are, after all, only human. One pick counsels another, and the next thing you know there is an empty plate, and when the man of the house returns after his few pints of porter and goes to the press for his piece of pig's head only a hard-hearted cynic could remain unmoved at the tragic expression of disappointment on his face.

For the development of neck muscles in children, the bone is recommended. It strengthens teeth and, although many may disagree with me, early enthusiasm for the jawbone has resulted in some excellent public house singers. If, during the meal, the conversation revolves about weighty issues, a man may chew on the pig's tongue and cogitate with advantage. If a man wants to drive home an observation, all he has to do to attract attention is to stick his fork into a sliver of lean meat and hold it aloft while he speaks.

Resentment becomes no man, but resentment is unavoidable when one listens to cheap music hall comments which endeavour to bracket the pig's head with louts and buffoons. Again, resentment rises when we hear of the denials of our boys and girls who leave home to work in the cities. All their lives they have known pigs' heads, eaten pigs' heads and relished pigs' heads, but fear of ridicule makes them ashamed to mention pigs' heads, and when the pig's head is drawn down derogatively they laugh with the rest as if they were above such vulgar indulgence, as if they had never been sent shopping by hardworking mothers, well instructed in the choosing of white-hearted cabbage and well versed in the characteristics of the better class halfhead. One can understand when young people deny the townlands of their upbringing and sing no longer of the hills of home, but there is no excuse for those who deny pig's head and cabbage. These are destined to live empty lives of pretence, and destined to occupy the positions of underlings regardless of the reward and responsibility of their positions, for a man who is ashamed of the simple pleasures of the past is neither a dreamer nor a builder. He is party to fraud because he will not be himself and he is easily led because betrayal and surrender are second nature to him.

On the other hand there is hope for the nation while we have young men who still insist on the old classic courses for dinner, young men who will not be easily duped or influenced, young men who will have no hesitation in resorting to physical redress at the least delineation of subjects which they have been reared to respect. They need have no fear of defeat because the subject of dispute is a bone-builder and a muscle-giver and a man after a meal of chicken and breadstuffing is at the mercy of the man who has dined on pig's head.

THIRTY

TOAST

SOME people haven't the faintest idea when it comes to making toast, not that the subject is worth much argument, but, if it is to be made at all, let it be made properly.

The electric toaster is an imbecile, a nincompoop, who knows as much about making toast as an elephant or a hippopotamus. Well-made bread is inserted into this infernal machine and reappears after a brief visit transformed into a discoloured anaemic old crone, unfit for the scandalous tables of monkeys, not to mention those of human beings.

Sometimes, in hotels, I have a mind to seize three or four slices of this particular variety of charcoal and stuff it into the pampered gobs of the conscienceless scoundrels who serve it. They have ruined a fairly respectable craft and despoliated a ritual as ancient as bread itself – because you cannot mass-produce toast. It must be made by hand, lovingly, and with an artist's eye for colour so that the more attractive shades of healthy brown may be arrived at. I always know, by the colour of the slices, how much care has been exercised in their making, and I won't be duped by hastily-made impostors, for their colouring is without depth and their tints without character.

Anyhow, what I would like to ask people in hotels is this – why all the toast? Do they think we are sick? Don't they know that toast is for invalids and old-age pensioners? You cannot dip toast in gravy and I defy anybody to chance mopping up the yolk of an egg with it. You can't fold toast and a man with his teeth out cannot tackle toast at all. A man with his teeth in is taking unnecessary chances. You can't break it and toss it into your soup. You dare not eat it in bed because its crumbs have the same effect as a colony of lunatic fleas. It must be eaten quickly or not eaten at all. Butter is no way far to go with it. Marmalade is utterly out of place on it. You can put sardines on it, you can put beans on it and as far as I can see you can put tapioca on it, but it is still toast. You can't make sandwiches out of it. You can't throw it to small birds on snowy mornings because they haven't a hope in the world of coping with it.

It is a dago. It isn't a biscuit and it isn't bread. It is no aid to the digestion. The vitamins have been roasted out of it mercilessly. You daren't eat it if you're wearing a decent suit of clothes because the butter deserts it for the sanctuary of a trousers or waistcoat. One wonders how it came into being at all. It must have been by accident. Some sated sybarite tossed a chunk of bread into a fire and an underling picked it out, dusted it, scraped it, tasted it, informed a master whose depraved stomach was constantly on the lookout for odd novelties, and it became a fad without rhyme or reason. It became fashionable. Centuries passed and another villain added marmalade to it. Who but a crackpot would think of marmalade on toast?

I will stick my neck out when I maintain that of all those who consistently breakfast on marmalade and toast, not a single one would honestly prefer it to good bread and farmer's butter. Can it compare with brown bread, mixed bread, soda bread, currant bread? Can it compete with any kind of bread? Yes, it can hold its own with burnt bread, for that is what it is. Under spaghetti it is strictly marshland, perfectly alright for those whose mouths are not peopled with teeth but abominable to those who are capable of grinding pork chops into fragments.

Toast rack is an apt title, for upon it the innocent slice of bread is tortured to death and subjected to such ignominious scorching, and transformation so hideous that the loaf from which it was taken would be hard put to recognise it. I will allow that there is a place for toast, but let us not lose sight of its proper niche in the vast world of edibles. Crusts are hard enough without making them any harder and it should not be forgotten that toast, after all, is a fellow who is not out of place in the company of Epsom Salts, castor-oil and senna leaves and there is enough to worry us in this world without being constantly reminded of the sick-room, so, if you please, I will have a few tasty slices of nice brown bread for my breakfast in the morning.

THIRTY ONE

OUR GRANDFATHERS

'Let us have him for his grey hairs.'
W. SHAKESPEARE

IT is not the craze for small boys to boast about their elders any more. Nowadays a grandfather is expected to behave like any other human being. He is an oddity if he sports whiskers, and a man with a doubtful background if he tells lies. It is fashionable to be ashamed if he is an oddity, and a character to be confined to his room if his mind wanders.

There was a time when elderly men were invested with the deeds of Robin Hood, and the prowess of Alexander. There was an age when small boys could ask impossible questions with impunity and be assured that an answer was forthcoming, even if it meant much plucking of moustaches and thoughtful thumbing of waistcoat pockets. When an embarrassing question is asked these days, there is the whispered mention of child psychiatry and a hurried change of subject. Nothing was beyond the range of an informed grandfather, and he made up for what he did not know by changing the subject subtly to one of his own choosing.

Once when a small boy asked a grandfather if John L. Sullivan was an acquaintance of his, it was intimated that the Boston Strong Boy had succumbed to the lethal left of said relative in a drinking-house which shall be left unnamed. Of course, there were real grandfathers in those days – men who had a nodding acquaintance with Sitting Bull, and who knew more about world crises than they were prepared to disclose.

They were, as a rule, men with stomachs of tremendous girth and protuberance, stomachs that wobbled precariously like blancmange when they hastened, and lent authority to statements which were laden with inaccuracy when they pontificated. They were men who could harrumph importantly like sea-lions, and frown like hippopotami. They were men of settled outlook, but they could be unpredictable, too, when it suited them.

They could wink imperceptibly at small boys who turned to look at the choir during Mass, and they could, without animosity, paralyze a streetful of disrespectful delinquents with a single paralysing glare. They sported genuine brass chains, and they possessed real turnip watches. They were, for the most part, men of few words. They were great artists, also.

They had, when called upon for a song, the grace to stand, moist-eyed and stricken, while they lamented the sad fate of an exiled maiden who expired inevitably upon a foreign shore. The veins would stand out on their faces like purple picture-cords, and globules of moisture would glisten on their foreheads. If a man of substance, such as Tony Weller, were present, he would most certainly have nodded discreet approval, turned his head to hide his feelings, and would most certainly have invited the author of the rendition to join him for a noggin of grog in the snug.

Please to remember that I am speaking about men who learned their art scientifically from tu'penny songbooks, men who scorned elocution, but who could quote by heart, under duress, every line and lament of 'Auburn' and the lesser-known stanzas of masterpieces like Gray's 'Elegy'.

Let the great strut stages for audiences who pay to hear them, but every day of the week give me the man who has the power to make his fellows turn away from porter, the power to quell with a regal sniff disturbances which might intrude upon their pronouncements, and the ability to impress their fellows by virtue of dignity alone.

There was a quality about men who could not bend to

tie their bootlaces. They were impervious to change. They clung to their fads. They demanded spare-ribs and turnips, when households turned against them. Let them be cruelly delineated by irascible artists, or exhibited on postcards with waxed moustaches and bulbous red noses, but I will not hear a word spoken against men who could hold a small boy rooted to the ground in admiration when they trumpeted fearlessly, like rogue elephants, into scarlet handkerchiefs.

They dressed soberly and conservatively, and they had regard for their suits. They wore waistcoats which were in continual danger of bursting, but, if an unreliable button popped occasionally like a champagne cork, comment was never made.

They viewed sportscoats and flannel trousers with contempt – the garb a man of dignity might associate with a frivolous ukulele-player at a doubtful seaside resort. They knew when a small boy felt insecure and lonely. They could dismiss marauding devils in the darkness with a familiar cough. They exuded confidence with calculated frowns, and they could place a penny in a child's hand with a ceremony which convinced the recipient that he was truly knighted. They could shave pencils better than carpenters and bring dubious metal to rapier points like farriers.

They did not die like old soldiers, and fade away. When they passed on it was said of them that their hearts had given out.

I salute the bulging waistcoats of yesterday – tobacco-perfumed parallelograms of pennied pockets!

THIRTY TWO

SOUP

'Let them that ate the mate, drink the soup!'
(OLD IRISH PROVERB)

ENTER any lounge-bar of your choosing and sit on a high stool. Place a trembling hand on your brow and complain of a sick head. It is odds on that a sympathetic barmaid will recommend anything from gin and tonic to brandy and advocaat. Other bar-stools will recite personal experiences and insist upon raw eggs and pale dry, or scotch cum pine-apple. Fools all! A man should hold on until lunch-time and take his chances with a plate of soup.

There was a time when a man called a spade a spade, and a restaurant an eating-house, when soup was a meal in itself and not a French aristocrat introducing a coterie of foppish relatives – a time when soup was a body-building necessity, thick enough to inscribe the initials of a lost sweetheart on its surface. I am speaking about soup, mind you – not broth. There is enough reticence in the world, and too much politeness.

There is the incident of a boy who complained about a hair in his soup. Are memories so curtailed that a grey hair from a mother's head may be forgotten with impunity, or is there to be a holocaust of denials altogether? Could we but now call back those beloved grey hairs of yesterday, no sacrifice would be too great and no price too exorbitant.

Go on! tell me that packeted, jacketed soups and canned soups are thick as gruel but you will not delude a man who knows that they can be processed the same as friar's balsam or calf's foot jelly. We live in an age of creme du this and creme du that, but how many remember *real* soup? the stuff that held as many surprises as a gross of lucky-bags and all the unpredictable possibilities of a Christmas uncle. How many are permitted to recall the real thing, the potent admixture where the remains of a rack chop could live in absolute harmony with a veal cutlet or a goose's gizzard?

We are a nation of die-hards and idealists. We will stand fast with the idea of democracy and defend the indefensible. Tragically, though, when it comes to soup we are as easily led as the rest. I am not preaching revolution. Let me make this clear at all costs. At the risk of impeachment, however, I commit myself, but throw myself on the mercy of men who had soupmaking mothers, men who not so very long ago sat at table with soupspoons upturned like oars and chubby childs' hands that hammered for soup.

Soup is no longer investigated. It is not even necessary to stir it any more, because there is little in it to stir. It is nowadays a preliminary bout. It can be done without. It is something towards which we have rather shamefully adopted a couldn't-care-less attitude. Surely to goodness it is as old as the pot, and its smell as ancient as the smell of smoke.

Far be it from me to belittle salad-cream or mustard. Allspice is for delicacies. I have nothing against it. Pinhead oatmeal, by all means, but do not saddle me with it. I can do without such things, but I cannot do without soup. Surely soup is as respectable as fish-paste and just as good as trifle, even if we are told otherwise. Or have we lost our sense of values altogether. Too many of the profound things in life are passing away. There is no more epic poetry. Plum puddings can be bought in shops, the same as hats. Plug tobacco is passing on, and small boys do not rob orchards any more. I heard yesterday of a boy who refused to eat early potatoes because they weren't peeled!

I will hold my tongue if I am elbowed accidentally in the midriff. I will count to ten – the same as the next fellow – if a man stands on my corns. But I draw the line when it comes to soup without bones. Here I suppress a bubble of diabolically sarcastic laughter because soup without bones is like a wedding without music, like a football match without a fracas, like her ladyship's lager without lime. Please do not smirk when I say that science has gone too far – that underfed, bespectacled counterfeiters have exceeded themselves. Forgive me if I say that serious consequences are inevitable. Pickled onions are not loved any more. Soup is merely a course!

Here is a question which I would like to put to medical gentlemen – have stomachs grown smaller? No need for immediate alarm, but it is something that bears thinking about when men sit down to concoctions in lavish catering-places, when they dip their spoons into that watery nonsense that flourishes under the proud title of soup.

THIRTY THREE

GOOSE'S BLOOD

IT is a free country and every man has a right to his say. He has also the right to walk away if he feels he is being imposed on. But still the wise man listens to everything, turns it over in his mind and forms a conclusion. Consequently, if the reader finds the title of this essay too sanguine for his taste he need not go further, but first I must tell him of a recent happening, adequately authenticated and vouched for by more than twenty two sober witnesses.

All I ask is a fair and impartial hearing. I think I am entitled to that.

In a not-too-distant city, the parents of a household were plagued morning, noon and night by the antics of their Teddy-boy son. He refused pork chops, beans and applesauce on a Monday. On Tuesday he cocked up his nose at Irish stew and spent three-and-fourpence on vanilla ice-cream. On Wednesday and Thursday they tried him with two differently-flavoured brown stews, only to hear him complain bitterly about both. On Friday he gave his mother a back-answer when she served him boiled cod for his lunch. On Saturday night he threw two straight lefts at his father, feinted with a right cross and flattened the unfortunate man with a left hook, and all because they gave him blackpuddings, sausages, kidneys and back-rashers for his supper. Instead of contributing to the upkeep of the home, he went out and bought two black shirts with tinsel buttons. He went to bed that night and we are not to be blamed if we conclude that he did not say his prayers.

On the Wednesday of the following week, his mother got a present of a goose from a sister who was married to a small farmer in Nenagh. The goose was delivered live by an elderly civil servant, female, who assisted in the killing of the bird. The bird was executed with a breadknife. The blood which flowed from the gaping wound in the back of the neck was captured in a white bowl. Salt was immediately added and the mixture stirred to prevent clotting. An onion was chopped fine and added. Stirring continued. Two tablespoons of flour, pinches of pepper and salt and one fistful of oatmeal completed the formula. The bowl containing the opulent concoction was put to one side for later use.

That night the youthful villain was at his worst. He threatened to leave home if the food did not improve. The mother was distracted. The father had left at the first sign of disturbance and the grapevine had it that he was seen drinking rum and peppermint in a distant tavern. The mother forsook her hearth to shed her tribulations upon the unresponsive ears of neighbours. The furniture was left unpolished and the shirts unironed. The Sunday chicken sat like a decaying corpse deprived of its stuffing. The pet, for such I am now about to call him, ranted and raved about the house seeking an outlet for his aggressive content. His eye settled upon an eggstand which contained an inoffensive egg spurned weeks before. He smashed container and contents against the wall but this was not enough. He seized a hanging print depicting a doe at dalliance with her fawn and flung it against the electric cooker. The glass fractured itself but the fauna though crumpled was still clearly visible. He roared abominations and challenged a neighbourhood of tired workmen from the sanctuary of his mother's kitchen. Luckily his challenges went unheard.

He sought further mischief and his eyes alighted upon the bowl of goose's blood. He seized it and raised it on high but some kindlier or more sensible instinct prevailed when the first whiff of soaked onion caught him. Tradition dies hard. Still filled with deviltry he sought and found a frying pan and was about to pour the contents of the bowl into its scintillating flats when the notion of dripping came to him. He found it in a lesser bowl and with his fingers scooped a quantity into the pan. He turned a knob on the cooker and immediately was doing business. The goose's blood, fortified by its constituents, sang its native songs and soon there was sizzling and puffing and finally a soft cake of irresistible brittleness was produced which he devoured without the aid of knife or fork. Like a mouse, he crept upstairs to bed and later when his scions sought their couch in the next room they wondered at his contented breathing.

Morning came and he ate the breakfast which a puzzled mother tendered. That night he returned from work wearing a corduroy trousers and a thirty-shilling sportscoat. His head was shaved to the bone and it wasn't because of Yul Brynner. From that day forward he was a model son and wound up his career by entering a monastic order where his good example was a credit to his upbringing.

So is it any wonder that I have little time for those who prefer banana fritters to goose's blood!

THIRTY FOUR

CURTAINS

IF you should pass a house with a broken window through which a bright curtain flutters gaily in the breeze, you may be sure that the house is full of small, noisy children, a spirited fraternity who are a full time job for a harassed young mother.

On the other hand, if the windows are hermetically sealed and boast no more than grey musty curtains it is a safe bet to say that the occupants of the house are as musty as the curtains.

If you pass a house with no curtains whatsoever on any of its windows one may conclude with reasonable certainty that the house is unoccupied; whereas with the house which has Venetian blinds you may rest assured that the owners are up and coming and doing well for themselves but on the other hand from a house which has purple curtains the very least you can expect is an Excise officer or a schoolmaster.

If you see a window with a curtain which is torn there can be no doubt but that the woman of the house is in the Nursing Home. Only a scoundrel or a troublemaker would tell her because it would spoil her rest and might result in giving the child a peculiar name which would embarrass it in later years.

Then there is the house with respectable curtains which have faded and need to be starched and replaced. I hesitate to tell you about this house because of the loneliness inside. Here you might find a greyhaired man whose wife has passed on and left him alone to fend for himself. He could, if he so wished, hire a housekeeper or have a woman in to tidy up, but you see he loved his wife with all his heart and he will never have another woman in the house because it would make him lonely for her and that would break his heart altogether.

Take the house which has curtains which are stained and soiled along the borders. I am not sure that I have any great love for those who occupy such a house because the chances are that the stains have been caused by fingers which are always parting the curtains when Paddy so-and-so is staggering home half-gattled from an overdose of porter or maybe to have a look so that the new style which appears on Sunday morning will provide a weekful of gossip for crusty old virgins who should have more sense for themselves.

I would not be too critical of curtains which do not match the house or the paint, because you will often see a man with a white face wearing a black hat, or a woman with red toenails wearing white sandals and anyway I will guarantee that the woman who runs such a house is absent-minded and forgetful but a first-class mother for all that and a woman who does not berate her husband when he has two up and one down in a win treble.

It is not always wise to be critical of a house which has gaudy curtains and it is neither just nor fair to judge the woman of the house by what is visible on the outside because the material of the exhibit in question may be a present from a pernickety mother-in-law or it is conceivable that the curtains were made from the makings of a slip bought in a fit of sudden abandon at a summer sale.

The ones from whom you can expect the most are bright colourful curtains because it is odds on that the couple inside are very much attached to each other and the only loud sounds which are ever heard from such a house are those of laughter and song.

Pink curtains are a reliable guide in the assessment of the woman who hung them. A wandering tramp with a sick head will almost always walk away from houses like this with the price of a cure in his breast pocket. I am not too keen on solemn ponderous curtains and while the owners may not be ponderous or solemn, they are not the type you would ask to join in a chorus of 'The Bould Thady Quill' on an excursion to Ballybunion.

Red curtains indicate a woman with a fiery temper and a husband with an active interest in blood sports. Multi-coloured curtains belong to people who indulge in active pursuits and it is possible that in such a house you might find a man who was second sub. for the local junior football team and a woman who plays Badminton once in a while.

Green curtains with white spots or polka dots remind me of apple-pies because of an old woman I knew when I was a small boy. It was her habit to invite me into her house and offer me a slice of apple-pie. Then she might ask me what my father was shouting about the night before or tell me that Mrs. Murphy was expecting again, or she would enquire with the utmost secrecy what we had for our dinner last Sunday. The more apple-pie she gave me the bigger the lies I told her.

Curtains with frills and other whatnots on to them belong to houses where blousy women rule the roost. These women may wear anything from three to five bangles and monstrous necklaces of imitation jewellery. These are rather showy people and they always give more than they can afford when a crowd of boys knock at the door collecting for a football or a diving-board.

Pale blue curtains are the curtains I like best of all because it is here that you will find a woman who is devoted to Our Lady and in such a house there is always a man who is a good warrant to tell stories about Red Indians and pirates and who will take a chap up on his lap when he comes home from work in the evenings and listen with the greatest attention to a small boy's momentous adventures during a hectic day.

THIRTY FIVE

HOLDING A MAN BACK

ONE of the least-extolled but most subtle of the lesser-known crafts is the art of holding a man back when he seems likely to endanger limb, life and ligament.

To the casual onlooker who is a peace-loving citizen by nature, the safest course under such uncertain circumstances is to take one's hands out of one's pockets and disappear swiftly from the scene. Much is lost by such thoughtless action.

For the man who shows the deeper interest in that which prompts the more violent emotions of his fellows there is a rich reward in spite of the risks involved, because, free of charge, he will be entertained by acting and mime of the most sensitive and delicate variety.

Years ago, at a horse-fair in a small country town, I was initiated as a member of that limited audience which is always to be seen wherever commotion is likely. The whole thing began over the sale of a three-year-old donkey. Unsupported claims about his breeding and staying-power were being questioned, and he, to his lasting shame, showed no interest whatsoever in the proceedings.

My attention was first attracted by several screaming women in shawls who ran wild-eyed through the fair, shouting: 'He's dead! He's dead!' and then more ingeniously: 'He'll be murdered! They have him killed stone dead!'

I hurried to the scene, to see a tall mountainy man with red hair, prancing violently like a stallion, his fists clenched, his chest expanded. There was white spume at the corners of his mouth and murder was very definitely glinting out of his fire-filled eyes.

'I'll tear the heart out of him!' he was shouting; 'I'll do

forty years in jail for him if I have to!'

The object of his wrath was a small fat man who wore a cap, and was held firmly by two grim six-footers who, between them, could have overpowered a four-year-old bull at their ease.

'Hold me back!' the red-haired man shouted. 'Hold me back, or I'll tear the windpipe out of him. I will! I'll do damage if I'm not held!'

Dutifully the pair, who had been restraining the small fat man, left him go, and acting upon instructions seized the red-haired man lest he carry out his terrible threats. This was the cue for the fat man. He flung his cap to the ground and danced on it. Women screamed and shrieked fervent aspirations. The fat man divested himself of his coat and crouched with a stance which would do credit to Marciano.

'I'll rip him open!' he screamed; 'I'll wallop the living daylights out of him!'

'He's the father of a family!' a voice pleaded from the circle of onlookers.

'I hope he has his will made,' said the fat man mercilessly, 'because he'll be on the flat of his back in a minute.'

More screams and imprecations, while the fat man circled his prey.

'Call the Guards!' some shouted; 'call the Guards before there's murder committed.'

The small man spat on his hands and lunged forward to fulfil his promises. His face was a frightful sight to behold but killing was narrowly averted when close associates, taking their lives in their hands, seized him and endeavoured to dissuade him.

'Let me go!' both parties shouted together.

It might have gone on indefinitely had not somebody shouted that a Civic Guard was approaching. The crowd quickly dispersed and the red-headed man took the reins of his donkey.

'What's going on here?' the Guard asked.

'An old woman got a fit,' said the red-haired man.

'That's right!' said the small fat man; "twas the bottled stout and she wasn't used to it.'

Occasionally, however, blows are unavoidable and litigation follows, but in ninety-nine cases out of a hundred the play is produced with no changes in the script and adjudicators' comments are not called for. Great credit is due, but rarely given, to the modest men who do the holding, and great technical skill is needed for this aspect of the presentation. A worried bloodless face can be extremely effective and can spread uneasiness and tension among inexperienced onlookers, but the great knack lies in letting a man almost go and then getting a grip on him again with what would seem to be a superhuman effort.

Woe to the player who does not abide by the rules and tries to come between the protagonists. It is almost certain that he will receive a sore head for his pains. In most places peace-makers are considered fair game for anybody who has a grudge against the world and youthful aspirants to the pugilist's trade are frequently encouraged to draw their first clouts at anybody foolish enough to intervene in what promises to be enjoyment of the first water.

The major artists, though, are the two who are held back and a missed cue by either one could end in disaster. The first indication of inaction to follow is when a man takes off his hat and dances on it. He is stalling for time and measuring the limitations of his foe. The more menacing the threats muttered, the less likelihood of bloodspilling. When he takes off his coat and throws it aside, we are well into the second act. When he rolls up his sleeves and spits on his hands the play is over and the shadows emerge from the wings to dim the footlights and draw the curtains upon the bowing players.

THIRTY SIX

DRISHEEN

DRISHEEN is not a village in Clare, nor the site of a new German factory in Kerry. Drisheen is one of our great national dishes, so great in fact that, once eaten, the taste remains in one's mouth for a lifetime. Pity those who prefer to vaunt about more expensive substances painted by the thin veneer of grandiose French, but thanks for him who wouldn't swop a ring of pig's pudding for all the bouillabaisse in Christendom.

I do not condone the action of a man who looks down his nose at those of lesser station, nor do I hold with those who believe themselves to be superior to others because of the accidental acquisition of material things. Snobbery I would outlaw and ostracism is not potent enough for those who affect the grand mannerisms of their momentary masters, but I hereby solemnly declare that a man with a plate of sausages should not be allowed to sit at the same table with a man who has a plate of drisheens.

There was a time when the butchering of a pig in a townland was a matter of tremendous consequence, not merely because it affected the palates of a dozen families but because there was a fierce partisan pride in the produce of every household, and the greatest epitaph that could be given a housewife might go like this: '*She may have been good or bad according to her lights, but she was a wonderful warrant to fill a pig's pudding.*' To those who have never tasted drisheen, the compliment will be meaningless, but to those who have further comment is not necessary.

There is a story I was once told, about an old man who lay on his sick-bed with all hope gone. Downstairs the family moved silently and spoke in hushed tones. The youngest offspring of a neighbour entered silently and respectfully with a parcel of puddings and porksteak from a freshly slaughtered pig. The table was laid and presently the puddings were hissing and sizzling in the pan. The unmistakeable aroma spread to the four corners of the house. A thump, followed by a loud prolonged wail, was heard from upstairs. Those in the kitchen crossed themselves, thinking the old man's hour had come. But no! – a moment later he thundered dangerously down the stairs in his nightshirt, the pallor gone from his face. He halted breathlessly and somewhat shamefacedly at the stair-foot. His plea was: '*In the honour o' God, keep one o' them puddin's for me!*'

There are a delicate set of rules to be observed when the porksteak is stripped from the carcase and the glowing rings of dark-brown drisheens sit eloquently in steaming tiers. A list which has been corrected and improvised for weeks is checked for the last time. None but tried neighbours, closest relatives and friends of long standing are included. From the children of the family a deliverer is chosen. He must have the stoic sufferance of a postman who does not carry the expected letter. He must be a boy with a natural talent for diplomacy. In other words he must know how many times he should refuse a half-crown before the final acceptance. He must be a boy with the innate skill of never letting his left hand know what his right is doing, and he must give the impression that every parcel is a special one. Tact and the true professionalism of a quartermaster-general are needed in the amount which must be apportioned to each family. Traditions cannot be disregarded in the light of sudden fancies and recent developments.

The inclusion of a few spare ribs in the right parcel could result in an alliance which might well weather the vagarious temperaments of generations. It is something greater than mere obligation, and to illustrate the importance of this point let us advance into the years and try to visualize a pair of hot young bloods about to engage in a fight to a finish. Older onlookers counsel peace. Others insist that they should be left at it. A ring is made and the antagonists assume the stance of pugilists. From the background and over the gulfs of time comes the voice of an elderly uncle. His words have a strange effect on the circle. '*Don't forget,*' he says, '*the night long ago they gave us the pig's liver!*' The youths look nonplussed, bewildered. Suddenly the contestants embrace. Great breeds of pigs are remembered – Landrace, Large White and Plain York. Other days and other joys are brought to mind. Men mumble soulfully about the heartlessness of a changing world and it is resolved that newly-acquired friends, hitherto unconsidered, shall not be forgotten when the next fat pig is due for slaughter.

Gone are the glimmering small girls with ribbons in their hair who cycled to town with a message-bag full for friends and relatives. They brought more than drisheens. They brought remembrance and the knowledge that loved ones are not forgotten when there is full and plenty. Around the table the gay household gathered. Worries about rates, insurances and bills went out the window and men with goodwill in their hearts saluted the providence of a Creator Who never for an instant forgets the dignity of simple people who know the real value of simple things. Gifts like these are given out of the goodness of men's hearts and it is heartening to think that there is at least one instance where money cannot deprive a man of his natural-born rights.

THIRTY SEVEN

MEN WHO HAVE ARRIVED

WHEN a chap reaches the age of four he has outgrown the stringent boundaries of his own backyard and, if the adventurous spirit burns strongly within him, he has made a number of expeditions to foreign places, such as rubbish-dumps and railway-stations. While he may have caused hearts to miss beats and search parties to be organised, he is, nevertheless, seen in a new light after his return, and regarded as a man who can be trusted up to a point in the handling of small business transactions.

I do not suggest for an instant that he is capable of taking sole charge in the matter of conveying a jug of sour milk from one house to another, but if there is nobody else around he might be sent downstairs on the morning of an August Bank Holiday to see if the paper is under the door.

Caution must constantly be applied, regardless of the triviality of the mission and under no circumstances should the gentleman under discussion be chosen to turn off the tap in the bathroom, or sent next door for the loan of a box of black polish. Men with little foresight have made disastrous errors through placing confidence prematurely in couriers who cannot be trusted to tie their own bootlaces.

Let us imagine a man in bed with a sick head, a tired body and an argumentative stomach. The wife discourages remedies of alcoholic content. The invalid has the wherewithal to make a discreet purchase but lacks the strength to do so. In desperation he enlists the aid of the youngest member of the household, who is entrusted with the money and a brief note which he is told to hand to a certain sympathetic barman in a familiar public-house.

With a miraculous combination of luck and chance, in one case out of a million he will do his job thoroughly and nobody will be any the wiser, but in all other cases he will unwittingly betray the sick man or, if not, he will most certainly break the bottle containing the cure. The very least he will do is uncork the bottle and sample its contents, in which case all is lost, and the unfortunate wretch in the bed is guilty of a crime for which there is no expiation and many a long day will pass before he will be allowed to forget his colossal misbehaviour.

Small boys are willing and eager to accept any task and the greater the lack of understanding in relation to the qualifications required, the greater is the desire to be involved. The training should begin with items like large individual turnips and sixpenny tins of beans. In the event of mishap, the loss in either case is not significant and should the messenger feel constrained to investigate purchases of this nature, his interest will quickly wane and there is some hope that he will deliver the goods.

To entrust the following articles to a small boy's care is to court trouble – ounces of pepper, ginger, cinnamon, allspice, ointment and caraway seeds; dozens of oranges, apples, eggs, beer and rhubarb; pounds of sugar, butter, tea, sausages and black-puddings; glasses, noggins, half-pints, pints and quarts of all known liquids.

To send two small boys, in the hope that one will succeed in counteracting the other, is fatal, since two small boys are capable of doing twice the damage of one. Beginners should never be cautioned about the importance of a commodity since this can only lead to pride and possessiveness and result in a small boy, without provocation, putting his message on the ground and challenging all-comers to a try in taking it from him. The only thing likely to suffer in the ensuing encounter is the message.

It is also important to remember that if there is an urgent need of a certain article, let us say mustard for the commander-in-chief's bacon, it is presumptuous to depend upon the speedy return of the small boy. Any one of the following will suffice to detain him – fresh puddles, drunken men, hay-cars, funerals, dog-fights, empty match-boxes and tin-cans, because whereas it may seem with these last that here is another small boy kicking another tin-can, it is in reality a brilliant young forward soloing through a swarm of awed backs in Croke Park. The problem here is that when the message is forgotten, there is no accounting for the presence of money when later he puts his hands in his pockets. He tries to remember but cannot be blamed if he does not tax his memory. A favourable decision is arrived at easily, for if the money was in somebody else's pocket it would be somebody else's money, wouldn't it? He therefore rightfully concludes that the money may be spent with limited impunity but his first feelings of commonsense tell him that if it is to be spent at all it is to be spent quickly.

If the just man falls seven times a day, then we may, in the parlance of good journalists, with certainty conclude, that a pound of steak will fall from the small boy's hands the same number of times, but whereas the just man does not pause to make retribution for his indiscretions, the small boy will use his handkerchief, his shirt and the tail of his coat to clean said meat, for, where the man is only afraid of his God, the boy is afraid of his mother. It is not fear precisely that impels him but fear of upsetting a situation of certainty which has contrived to feed, clothe, warm, protect and entertain him since the day he was born.

A boy who has not broken eggs and spilled milk in his brief lifetime is not a boy in the strict sense. A boy is somebody who has the ability to smuggle a halfbottle of gin and a dozen of stout through an impassable upstairs back window when unexpected visitors arrive. A boy is also somebody of a different dye who can effectively kick the door of a drowsing chemist for a repeat of his grandmother's stomach bottle at all hours of the morning and a boy is somebody whose eyes will cloud and whose jaw will jut forward when he hears of injustice in the diminutive world of men.

Some may laugh when he first begins to belabour his hair with guaranteed hair-cream; others may snicker when he searches vainly for an early harvest of hairs on a jaw which is only thirteen years old, but if real despatch is needed where errands are concerned, all that is required is to send him off on a bicycle with directions, and where professionals will perish he will survive, to show that there is Somebody somewhere Who has an interest in boys of all shapes, sizes and kinds.

THIRTY EIGHT

LING

In the days when baker's bread was a luxury and our grandmothers sat in carts holding their donkeys in terror of steamrollers, there were men whose likes will never walk the earth again.

Long before rainbow trout usurped the rights of innocent and familiar tenants in our inland waters and before the first pony shied at the blast of a saxophone, there were men in Kerry whose big hands could pull a currach to safety or play a tune on a fiddle that would put a mountainy lark to shame, men who caught balls in Croke Park with one hand and with the other made ample room for a clearance as dignified as it was stylish, men who when they kicked a ball would turn around and start a conversation with the goal-keeper, resting assured that the affairs of the world would be put in order before the leather had landed safely behind the white lines of the foe.

To hell with devilled eggs, where they belong, and preserve us from marmalade on toast. We have nothing against boloni and spaghetti, but we resent imposition. Put a couple of pounds of Ling steeping in common water and we will give no trouble, because Ling is the stuff that gave the backbone to our fathers and inured them against the buffetings of wind and rain. Sit down, if you want to, and make a fool of yourself over grilled salmon and the knick-knacks that make it palatable, but do not preach a gospel to us for we are sick to the gills of innovation.

Volumes could be written about Ling and odes composed to it but you need to have it in front of you smothered in its own sauce with well-bred potatoes and a good skelp of fresh butter dissolving delightfully while you say a short prayer in thanksgiving for the good things in life that come for next to nothing.

Life, as the song says, is 'a weary puzzle', but there is no problem with Ling so long as there is enough to go round, and the year has been a good one for potatoes. Ling is the food of men whose stomachs have not been found wanting, whose digestive tracts are the envy of anatomists, whose hearts are the hearts of giants and whose strength is the fathomless strength of men who regard noodle-soup as baby-food.

Sausages and mash and fish and chips have played their part in assuaging the pangs of hunger, and only a churl would deny the claims of onion-dip and potato cakes but man must go deeper if he is to find the answer to honest hunger and the rewards of honest toil. Rashers have played giddy tunes on countless frying pans, and kettles have whistled melodies that would leave the Top Twenty in the shade, but there is a richer music with a deeper meaning and you get it only when you lift the cover from the pot where Ling is boiling. Here is the depth of the ocean itself and in the throaty gurgle of the bubbling sauce is the history of mariners who scorned the Atlantic when Columbus was teething and Amerigo Vespucci playing marbles in the alleyways of Italy. Here is all the sibilance of salt-laden breezes and the malicious chuckling of eddying water in pools where the devil-fish lurk, and here is an aroma that could transform an articulate man, the essence of composure and sobriety, into a gibbering fool who will be appeased by nothing unless it is a dinner of Ling on his plate. We read of the Spartan boy whose stomach was eaten away by a fox-cub, safe in the knowledge that it could never happen to a youth fortified and hardened by Ling for no fox could penetrate the muscle that it forms.

Ah, but tragically to-day there is an element, a class that will have nothing to do with Ling. I have seen them pass by the doorways where the flitches hang invitingly, cocking their noses into the air and swinging their nylon-mesh shopping-bags as if they were passing through the native quarter in Casablanca. I have seen them passing in their two-toned motor-cars and what harm but they're never very far away from Ling and who knows but one day they might haggle like fishwives over its purchase and be glad to sit down where Ling is the order of the day. I have seen them with suede coats and hair-do's executed by imported contortionists and I have listened to them deploring the absence of brill and turbot, or baby-beef if it wasn't Friday, and I would like to ask them – what is the matter with Ling. I would appreciate a definitive defence of their sad preferences.

The rafters in the thatched houses of your grandfathers were never without a flitch of it, and when your Auntie Mary came back from America 'twas the first thing she asked for. Bishops and Monsignors were reared on it and it was responsible for the pointing of more fifties than sirloin steak and raw eggs put together.

A word to mothers! Give them Ling when they're growing and they'll never lose the tooth for it and maybe they'll never be ashamed of the county that gave them birth or the sagas of their ancestors. But a word of warning! Ling is not for the immature or the unitiated. Don't give it to Teddy-boys or Kerrymen with Cockney accents for if you do the hair will stand erect on their heads and all the hair-oil in the world won't flatten it again, but if you have a lad with a likely pair of hands and the indelicate instincts of a full-back give him Ling when he's young and maybe one day that is the terrible man you'll see in Croke Park coming out of a swarm of forwards with the ball in his hands and a horrible expression on his face.

You don't need a cookery book for Ling because there is only one method of cooking. Put enough of it down and that way nobody will be disappointed when distribution

takes place. Forwards were never discouraged or kept at
bay by banana sandwiches and last-minute goals were
never scored by men whose mothers were slaves of the
frying pan. You don't see penalties stopped by hands that
were moulded by biscuits and sweet cake. Ling is the thing
that brought the crowd to its feet and swelled the hearts of
supporters when the day seemed lost. Hardy hats and
hobnailed boots may be disappearing but there is still hope
for the family that is not ashamed of Ling. Let its enemies
say what they will and let dieticians have the last word but
when the shouting is over we'll go home to our dinners and
we won't be swayed by the opinions of those who think they
know what is good for us. The best judge of the food fittest
for our development is the stomach that has to digest it and
the pocket that has to pay for it. When our emigrants
boarded the suicide craft that took them across the Atlantic,
it wasn't tomatoes or tinned pears they took with them.
Only the improvident embarked without a few flitches of
Ling. Tomatoes are all very fine for vegetable soup, but
when there was a wind from the northeast and ice in the
spume a man with tomatoes had as much chance of survival
as the old grey mare at the battle of Balaclava.

Let the Russians boast of a better way of life and let the
Chinese send their rice in showers around the world but let
it be remembered that there was Ling before them and there
will be Ling after them. Let the big powers debate the likelihood of the world's end and measure the force of their
bombs but a man with dry turf and a couple of flitches of
Ling on his ceiling has little to fear from the vanity of dema-
gogues or the threats of dictators.

Ling needs no aperitif but if there's buttermilk handy, a
mug or two is recommended before and during the meal.
As an aftercourse you may dispense with the habitual jellies
and puddings, because Ling leaves room for nothing more
but I have been told on reliable authority that a few pints

of well-conditioned stout a few hours later is acceptable, after which a man may retire for the night and sleep the sleep of the just.

I have been told that the best way to steep Ling is in a gallon of sour milk, where it should be left for twenty-four hours. I have never tried it, and would not recommend it for it is too valuable a commodity to be subjected to dubious experiment.

In conclusion I can only say that if we are not careful to foster a love of Ling among the youth of the country, one of our great national dishes will soon be regarded as the dish of squares and banned forever from the tables where it held sway since the first small-boat was manned and men looked for their dinners in the ocean.

LETTERS OF AN IRISH PARISH PRIEST
John B. Keane

There is a riot of laughter in every page and its theme is the correspondence between a country parish priest and his nephew who is studying to be a priest. Father O'Mora has been referred to by one of his parishioners as one who 'is suffering from an overdose of racial memory aggravated by religious bigotry.' John B. Keane's humour is neatly pointed, racy of the soil and never forced. This book gives a picture of a way of life which though in great part is vanishing is still familiar to many of our countrymen who still believe 'that priests could turn them into goats.' It brings out all the humour and pathos of Irish life. It is hilariously funny and will entertain and amuse everyone.

LETTERS OF A MATCHMAKER
John B. Keane

These are the letters of a country matchmaker faithfully recorded by John B. Keane, whose knowledge of matchmaking is second to none.

In these letters is revealed the unquenchable, insatiable longing that smoulders unseen under the mute, impassive faces of our batchelor brethren.

Comparisons may be odious but readers will find it fascinating to contrast the Irish matchmaking system with that of the 'Cumangettum Love Parlour' in Philadelphia. They will meet many unique characters from the Judas Jennies of New York to Finnuala Crust of Coomasahara who buried two giant-sized, sexless husbands but eventually found happiness with a pint-sized jockey from North Cork.

LETTERS OF A LOVE-HUNGRY FARMER
John B. Keane

John B. Keane has introduced a new word into the English language — 'chastitute'. This is the story of a chastitute, i.e. a man who has never lain down with a woman for reasons which are fully disclosed within this book. It is the tale of a lonely man who will not humble himself to achieve his heart's desire, whose need for female companionship whines and whimpers throughout. Here are the hilarious sex escapades of John Bosco McLane culminating finally in one dreadful deed.

LETTERS OF AN IRISH PUBLICAN
John B. Keane

In this book we get a complete picture of life in Knockanee as seen through the eyes of a publican, Martin MacMeer. He relates his story to his friend Dan Stack who is a journalist. He records in a frank and factual way events like the cattle fair where the people 'came in from the hinterland with caps and ash-plants and long coats', and the cattle stood 'outside the doors of the houses in the public streets.'

Through his remarkable perception we 'get a tooth' for all the different characters whom he portrays with sympathy, understanding and wit. We are overwhelmed by the charms of the place where at times 'trivial incidents assume new proportions.' These incidents are exciting, gripping, hilarious, touching and uncomfortable.

Send us your name and address if you would like to receive our complete catalogue of books of Irish Interest.

THE MERCIER PRESS
4 Bridge Street, Cork, Ireland